MASSACRE CREEK

'Bloody Khuyper' they called the captain who ruled the Union Army's prisoner-of-war camp in the west. And no Johnny Reb hated the man more than Sabin Shay of Texas. When word came that Khuyper was to command an expedition against the hostile Indians, Sabin Shay saw his chance. He disavowed the Confederacy, swore allegiance to the Union and volunteered to fight Indians as a 'Galvanized Yankee,' knowing that Khuyper would make his life hell on the trail and knowing that his name would come up for every suicide patrol...

MASSACRE CREEK

Gordon D. Shirreffs

ATLANTIC LARGE PRINT
Chivers Press, Bath, England.
Curley Publishing, Inc.,
South Yarmouth, Mass., USA.

Br 4/91

Library of Congress Cataloging-in-Publication Data

Shirreffs, Gordon D.
  Massacre Creek / Gordon D. Shirreffs.
    p. cm.—(Atlantic large print)
  ISBN 0–7927–0071–6 (soft: lg. print)
  1. Cheyenne Indians—Fiction. 2. Dakota Indians—Fiction.
3. Large type books. I. Title. II. Series.
[PS3569.H562M36 1990]
813′.54—dc20   89–23431
                                                            CIP

British Library Cataloguing in Publication Data

Shirreffs, Gordon D. (Gordon Donald)
  Massacre creek.
  I. Title
  813′.54 [F]

  ISBN 0–7451–9663–2
  ISBN 0–7451–9674–8 pbk

This Large Print edition is published by Chivers Press, England, and
Curley Publishing, Inc, U.S.A. 1990

Published by arrangement with Donald MacCampbell, Inc

U.K. Hardback ISBN 0 7451 9663 2
U.K. Softback ISBN 0 7451 9674 8
U.S.A. Softback ISBN 0 7927 0071 6

Photoset, printed and bound in Great Britain by
REDWOOD BURN LIMITED, Trowbridge, Wiltshire

MASSACRE CREEK

FOREWORD

There are persistent frontier legends about Confederates who refused to surrender after Appomattox. Some of General Joe Shelby's men moved through Texas after the war, living off the state, several thousand un-reconstructed Rebels, going to Mexico to offer their sabers to Maximilian. Some got through.

Somewhere in Sonora, on the lonely Mesa of the Bellmaker, there are two families descended from Confederates who had left the United States after the Civil War rather than take the oath of allegiance. Their intermarried descendants speak no English.

There is a tale from the Powder River country of Wyoming. It tells of a column of thin gray-clad ghosts who followed the bloody Bozeman Trail up into Montana in the summer of 1865 and settled there. Whether they were ghosts or living men we do not know. The answer has been lost through the passage of time. But they were *Confederates.*

Perhaps there were men like Sabin Shay and his 'Galvanized Yankees'. Quien sabe? Who knows?

CHAPTER ONE

The dry west wind scurried across the barren earth of Kansas and rattled grit like buckshot against the warped walls of the prison hospital. The sun had died long ago in a welter of rose and gold to the west and the new moon had not risen to soften the harsh landscape. The noise of the wind sounded like the scrabbling of bony fingers to Sabin Shay as he wiped the sweat from his face and looked across the body of the dead boy at Surgeon Hamish Hume, late surgeon, Provisional Army of the Confederacy.

Hamish Hume scratched his lean jaw with stained fingers. 'Putrid blood,' he said quietly, his soft burr hardly apparent. 'A common after-effect of erysipelas. The disease got into the bloodstream, Sabin.'

Sabin Shay passed a big hand through his thick dark hair. He looked down at the wasted body of his kid brother. 'This damned Yankee prison,' he said hoarsely. 'Miles might have had a chance if that bastard Khuyper hadn't kept him so long in that guardhouse cell.'

The surgeon shrugged. He eyed the broad-shouldered man across from him, noting the dark circles beneath the hard gray eyes. 'Aye, But it was only a matter of time.

1

We did all we could.'

Sabin drew the sweat-soaked sheet across the drawn face of the dead boy. 'Yeh! Muriated tincture of iron, alternated with quinia and emulsion of flaxseed. God!'

Hume washed his capable hands in carbolic solution. 'You need rest, Sabin. You've been on duty here for twenty-four hours. There was nothing else you could do.'

Sabin smashed a big right fist into his left palm and looked about the little improvised prison hospital. It was tenanted by the agonized bodies of his men. A full quarter of the old cavalry company fought various stages of erysipelas, typhus, typhoid and enteric fever. Two typhus cases had died of pneumonia that very day while Miles Shay fought the last long battle for life. The guttering candle lanterns cast alternate sweeps of shadow and light over the sick men. The mingled stench of carbolic, raw wood, sweat and fecal matter hung in the room like a miasma.

'Filthy,' Sabin Shay said. 'Rotten food. A few piddling medical supplies. That Yankee bastard is trying to kill us off. Why don't he line us up and execute us? Get it over with! Three months now, Hamish. Three whole stinking months of this! All because we fought his damned volunteers to a standstill and put a slug through his shoulder. I know what to do!'

2

The lean surgeon wiped his hands and leaned against the wall. 'You could have been sent to the officers' prison at Alton, Illinois. You might have been exchanged or paroled by now.'

Sabin's hard eyes held the blue ones of the Scot. 'You know why I ripped the bars from my collar and the braid from my sleeves. I couldn't let the kid come here alone. Before God, if I'd known this was going to happen I would have fought to the last with my bare hands. But Miles was wounded. I *had* to stay with him! Khuyper killed him here the same as if he'd gunshot him!'

Hume put on his faded gray coat. 'No. The war killed the boy. He was worn out from poor food and exposure before he was captured. The wound was dangerous. It welcomed disease into his body. The boy was doomed.'

Sabin walked to the door, seeking a change in air. His hands opened and closed spasmodically. He looked across the little prison compound, past the barracks, almost as though he could see through the high pine wall into the quarters where Captain Frank Khuyper sat at his ease.

A deep-toned infantry G bugle sounded out on the parade ground of little Fort MacNaughton. The wind was cold but it did whisper of the vast plains to the west. Of Kansas, Nebraska, Wyoming and Utah. The

3

country Sabin Shay knew and loved so well. It also whispered ghoulishly of what Sabin Shay would do to Captain Khuyper.

Floor boards creaked as Surgeon Hume came up behind Sabin, carrying with him the fused odors of carbolic and strong tobacco. 'The boy might have been killed by Kiowas or Comanches in some unnamed skirmish. Disease is prevalent in the Confederate forces. One way or another he might have died. It was in the throw of the dice, Sabin.'

'I'm still alive.'

Hume nodded. 'You've got a constitution like a grizzly. Your years on the plains made a strong man of you. The boy was a scholar, a musician, too delicate for the rough life.'

Sabin shook his head. 'He wanted to serve with me. He was a mere kid when I went to New Mexico with Sibley. I was just a sergeant then, but when I came home to convalesce from the wound I got at Valverde, I had lieutenant's bars on my collar. He was all for enlisting right away. I prevented him. Then I received orders to form an independent company for service against the Kiowas and Comanches. He showed up at our camp on the Pease River, hot as hell's fire to enlist. I ordered him home but he swore he'd enlist elsewhere. He was old enough. I had to take him.'

'He had a lot of you in him, Sabin. You were younger than he was when you went

4

west to fight Indians. Tell me? What did you expect from a Shay?'

Lantern light glistened from the polished rifle barrel of a sentry as he paced the catwalk above the big compound gate. Power seemed to flow down to Sabin's hands from his broad shoulders. He felt as though he could easily scale that wall, smash the sentry into a bloody jelly, and then go to find Khuyper.

'I'll not be here much longer,' the surgeon said quietly. He raised his face to let the cold wind dry the sweat which dewed it.

'You're taking advantage of General Order Sixty?'

'No. Surgeons can be released without exchange or parole through an agreement between the two governments.'

'You'll go back to Texas?'

Hume hesitated. 'No.'

Sabin eyed him. 'So? What are you driving at?'

Hume felt for a cigar and lit it. The quick sulphurous burst of the lucifer accentuated the planes of his face. 'I've been asked to take the oath of allegiance to the United States.'

Sabin leaned forward. 'You won't do that!'

Hume shrugged. 'I'm not a fire-eating Rebel, Sabin. I'm still a British subject. I could just as easily have joined the Union forces in the beginning. It so happened I was in Texas at the time, and was carried away by good whiskey and noisy local patriotism. I've

5

regretted my decision.'

'I can't believe it of you.'

Hume eyed his cigar appreciatively. 'A doctor is dedicated to the service of humanity, whether they wear blue or gray clothing.'

'A damned Galvanized Yankee!'

'Call it what you will. I plan a long life dedicated to help the suffering, Sabin. The war has been on almost four years. The Confederacy is fighting a losing battle. They're doomed.'

'We're not licked!'

'No?' The surgeon smiled wryly. 'There speaks the stout heart. But the facts are as plain as the long Scottish nose on my face. New Orleans fell in '62. Gettysburg and Vicksburg broke the back of the Confederacy back in '63. The Federal blockade has strangled Confederate commerce. It's a lost cause, my bitter friend.'

'God,' Sabin said. 'Coming from you—'

'I'm a canny Scot. I can see the handwriting on the wall. One hundred and twenty years ago my people learned a bitter lesson at Culloden. They fought well. They always do. But they were outnumbered, facing finely equipped troops and lots of artillery. Courage and blood could not sway the balance, and God knows, they had more than their share of that. There is a striking similarity between them and the South.'

6

'You'll be executed if the Confederates capture you in a bluebelly uniform.'

'The odds are against it. I'm not staying here, nor am I going back to the States. The Federals need surgeons along the Oregon Trail. That's where I'm heading.'

Sabin looked away. Hamish Hume was one of the few men he had ever met in his wandering life who seemed to fit into Sabin's idea of real friendship. Now the quiet Scot had destroyed the one worthwhile thing Sabin had found at Fort MacNaughton. With Miles dead, and Hamish gone, there would be nothing left at the fort but the bitter days and the lonely nights. Marianne Bascomb had not written from New Orleans since his imprisonment months ago. There was nothing left now but his hate for Frank Khuyper.

'One more thing,' Hamish Hume said as he flicked the ashes from his long nine. 'I've been promised that I will never be used against the Confederate forces; only against the Indians on the frontier, with the Federal forces holding them in check along the Oregon Trail. It should be interesting.'

'A Yankee trick.'

'No. I might add that the Federals are anxious to have Rebel prisoners take the oath of allegiance for service against the Indians. You could do it, Sabin. You know the Plains Tribes better than most men. How about it?'

'Go to hell, you turncoat bastard!'

Hume threw away his cigar. 'You're overwrought, Mr. Shay! I'll overlook that remark. Get some sleep. You're wasting precious health.' The surgeon turned on a heel and strode away.

Sabin walked into the reeking hospital. He stopped by the cot of Driver Ellis, a rawboned trooper from the banks of the Neches. The foul odor of excrement clung about Sabin as he eased the big man over and patiently cleaned the filth from him as if he were a child.

'Galvanized Yankee,' he muttered.

Driver opened his lusterless eyes. 'Yuh say Yankee, Cap'n Shay, suh?'

Sabin nodded. 'Take it easy, Driver.'

The lantern light showed the fiery acrid humor of erysipelas on the head and face of the big man. St. Anthony's Fire was what Hume called the characteristic rose rash. That was like Hume, to have a name which fitted everything like a glove, in his precise, logical mind. Hume had a solution for everything. His decision to take the Federal oath of allegiance had been the result of his cold logic. A logic that filled Sabin with more disgust than the excrement on his hands.

CHAPTER TWO

The men of Shay's Independent Frontier Company stood with bared heads, leaning against the strong cold wind. The early morning sun was a cold globe in the cloudless sky. The post cemetery was on a slope overlooking the waters of the Smoky Hill. A curious Kansas Indian sat his gaunt pony across from the cemetery, and then whipped it into motion as he saw the raw pine box being lowered into the grave.

Trooper Blalock Lott, a backslidden sinner who had once been an elder of the Campbellites, raised his thin hands and looked upward, speaking in a gravelly voice. The words of the Twenty-Third Psalm cut across the murmur of the wind. Sabin picked up a clod as Lott finished, and crumbled it into the grave. One after the other, the remaining members of Shay's Company crumbled earth atop the coffin of Trooper Miles Shay.

Sabin turned away. 'Sergeant Kester,' he said, 'mark it in the book. Private Shay, Miles, from Duty to Died of Disease in prison.'

Sabin strode away, never looking back, but the clear ring of the shovels and the hollow thumping of the clods on the pine box followed him to where the guards leaned on their long Springfields, watching the ragged Confederates bury another of their dead.

There were now eleven graves in the little prison cemetery. Sabin remembered them all. Donaldson, Doxmude, Fettis, Fischer, Kleinschmidt, Moss, O'Hara, Olney, Pratt, Wolfe and Shay. How many more of them would lie there before the rest gained their freedom? Many of the company had been killed or seriously wounded in the bloody little fracas at Badwater Creek. Sabin's orders had been to pursue and attack a raiding party of Kiowas which had come down on the Pease in the light of a late fall moon. They had struck the Kiowas near Badwater Creek, and had scattered them, killing half of them, but Shay's Company had suffered too.

Sabin's men had been short of ammunition when they ran into a strong reconnaisance force of Kansas Volunteers. John Easterly, Sabin's second-in-command, had been downed. A giant Yankee had bayoneted the wounded officer and pitchforked him over his head. Sabin's last pistol shot had smashed the killer's face into a red jelly. Miles went down with a terrible wound. There had been nothing to do but to surrender to the strong Yankee force.

There were times when Sabin wished he had fought to the death, ripping with teeth and claws, to end up buried in an unmarked grave beside John Easterly. But Sabin had ripped the bars from his collar and the braid from his sleeves and surrendered as an enlisted man so as not to be separated from Miles.

Sabin waited for his men and marched with them into the compound. He looked back over his shoulder just before the gate closed behind them. A tall officer was standing on the porch in front of headquarters, watching them. The wind ruffled the silken blond hair which he wore in a long cut.

'That cold-eyed Yankee sonofabitch,' said Little Warner Giddings, Sabin's company trumpeter.

'I'd like to get my hands on him,' said gaunt Norton Fraser. 'No Comanche would beat me in torturing *him*.'

The gate slammed shut behind them and the sentry yelled down from the catwalk. 'Scatter, you Rebel bastards!'

'Hell with you!' Giddings yelled back.

The guard cocked his Springfield. 'I'll put a ball through your belly!'

Giddings grinned. 'Never saw a Yank yet that could hit a man from that range.'

'Shut up,' Sergeant Kester said. 'Yuh might get fooled.'

Sabin went into the barracks while the prisoners policed the compound. Miles' empty bunk still stood beside the window, next to Sabin's bunk. Sabin took the battered

11

tin box from beneath his brother's cot. The lid was awry. Sabin had locked it the night he took Miles to the hospital. The lock had been pried open. He flipped back the bent lid. The little roll of shinplasters was gone, as well as the lone goldpiece. The silver-chased claspknife was gone too. It had been a gift from laughing Sally Ross, the girl who had kept Miles' heart back in San Antone; the girl who had stitched the company's swallow-tailed guidon with the Star of Texas on it. Miles had been guidon bearer, almighty proud of the crossed flags sewn just above the elbows of his shell jacket. And that guidon had singled Miles out for the Yankee bullets on the Badwater.

Big Matt Duggan came into the barracks. It was like him to loaf while the others did their share of the policing. Duggan dropped on his bunk and laced thick fingers behind his dirty reddish hair. Sabin placed the battered tin box on his bunk and stared at the big trooper.

'Sure sorry about Miles,' Duggan said loudly.

Sabin nodded.

'That little Ross filly back in San Antone will shore take it hard.'

If I find that knife on you, Sabin thought, I'll break your thick neck like a matchstick.

One by one the prisoners drifted into the cold barracks. No firewood had been issued

12

for several days, although the post woodyard was well stocked with it. The men all came in except little Phin Harris. Kester tapped the roster book with a dirty fingernail. 'I entered it, sir,' he said.

'*Sir*,' Duggan mimicked.

Kester whirled. 'We agreed that Cap'n Shay would keep command here,' he said.

'Bull chips,' Duggan said as he excavated a bit of breakfast sowbelly from between his stained teeth.

Kester glanced angrily at Sabin. Sabin shook his head. Kester was an old Regular who had served in Texas and New Mexico before the war.

'We're a-dyin' here like flies,' Duggan said morosely. 'Driver Ellis ain't got long to go. When do we get exchanged, Kester?'

Kester shrugged. 'Damned if I know. What about it, sir?'

'There's some slip-up,' Sabin said. 'They claim we're not regular troops of the Confederacy. I tried to write to Texas for confirmation. The letter was kept here in the files.'

'That bastard Khuyper again,' Kester said.

'I could'a been in the Fifth Texas in Virginia,' Duggan said. 'Them's the fightin' fools of the Lone Star State.' He looked at Sabin. 'I gotta get drunk and end up in *this* outfit. Shay's Independent Frontier Company! Jeesus!'

13

'Yuh would'a had yore butt shot off at Antietam or somewheres,' Warner Giddings said.

'What the hell does a windjammer like you know about war?' Duggan yelled.

Giddings spat. 'I'd like to wrap that ole horn around yore dirty neck, Duggan.'

A half mad light flickered in the pale green eyes of Matt Duggan as he sat up. 'I got bobcat bristles on my belly,' he said ominously. 'I'm an eye-gouger an' a fighter from who laid the chunk. Anyone here wanna try me?'

'Shut up,' Norton Fraser said. He squatted beside Sabin. 'We got to get outa here, Cap'n Shay,' he said. 'If'n we don't, we'll all be a-killin' each other afore the Yankees do.'

'I know,' Sabin said quietly.

Fraser scratched in his ragged beard. 'Now I figger it thisaway: Jump the guards some dark night. Take their guns. Break for the corrals to get hosses.'

'Then what?' Kester asked.

'Head for the Arkansas.'

'The country's alive with Kiowas and Comanches. The Yanks got posts all over.'

'We kin travel at night.'

'With troops from half a dozen places on our tail? You're loco.'

'Damn it, Kes!' Fraser said hotly. 'Yuh want to join them boys in the cemetery?'

'Hell no!'

14

'Then let's talk business.'

It was the old routine. Talk about impossible escapes to keep their minds from rotting like their bodies. Between the well fed, splendidly equipped Yankees and the bloodthirsty Kiowas and Comanches, they didn't have a tinker's chance in hell.

'Yuh ain't said much, Cap'n Shay,' Fraser said.

Sabin closed the tin box. 'You know the odds.'

'What about headin' west?' Corporal Lockerby asked.

'More Injuns,' Fraser said.

Duggan yawned. 'Dirty, thievin' scum,' he said. 'We could go through 'em like a dose of Glauber's Salts. They ain't no match for Texicans.'

Sabin eyed the big man. 'The Pawnees have enlisted as Yankee Scouts along the Oregon Trail,' he said. 'Beyond them are the Teton Sioux and the Cheyennes, and the Arapahoes are no cinch either.'

Duggan's thick lips curved in a slow sneer. 'I forgot yuh was an expert on Injuns,' he said. 'How are them Cheyenne squaws anyways?'

Sabin went white. Duggan knew more than Sabin had expected.

Kester cursed. 'I'll take him on,' he said.

Duggan sat up again and flexed huge muscles. 'Come on, Kes. I'll change that ugly

15

face of yourn.'

Sabin got to his feet. 'Forget it, Kester,' he said. 'We'll settle nothing by fighting amongst ourselves.'

'Yes, sir.'

'*Yes, sir,*' Duggan mimicked. 'My God!'

Sabin felt cold sweat run down his sides. It was only a matter of time before Duggan irked someone into a bloody rough-and-tumble, and Sabin wasn't so sure he could take the big man. Sergeant Tim Downey had tangled horns with Duggan their first week in prison. Duggan had beaten him to a pulp. His wounds had brought on the erysipelas which had eventually sent him to his grave.

'You're due for hospital orderly,' Sabin said to Duggan.

Duggan grinned. 'I ain't goin' in *that* pesthole. Turn or no turn. Get some other damn fool to go.'

Sabin looked about the room. The drawn faces avoided his. It was always so. 'I'll go,' he said. He walked outside into the cold wind, hating the thought of going to the hospital, but disliking the tension in the barracks still more.

CHAPTER THREE

Surgeon Hume looked up from his desk in the little office. 'Where's Duggan? We need wood and water.'

'I'll get it,' Sabin said. 'Duggan refused to come. That man's a real troublemaker.'

'I know.' Hume plucked at his long lower lip. 'What's wrong, Sabin? Are they talking escape again?'

Sabin nodded.

'The bloody fools. None of them is in condition.'

'Well, it keeps their minds off their troubles.'

Hume leaned back in his chair. 'Phin Harris is working as mess orderly in the officers' mess,' he said a bit too casually.

'So?'

'I ate there this morning, Sabin. At the invitation of Major Donaldson. He's from the Military Division of the Missouri. From the Inspector General's Department.'

Sabin waited, frowning, puzzled. Hume cleared his throat.

'You may as well know, Sabin. Phin Harris took the oath this morning. He's volunteered to fight Indians.'

First there was a shock, because one of the men had given in to the Yankees. And then

Sabin realized that it was only Phin Harris. He broke into a grin.

'He'll be a great help,' he jeered. 'Hell, it's an omen that the Indians have the sign on the Feds. Signing up Phin Harris. My God, how hard up can they get?'

Hume relit his cigar. 'I'll have to agree on Harris. But—'

'You, though. You're still going through with it, Hamish?'

'I am,' Hume purred, and then Driver Ellis raised his huge, shaggy head from his pillow. 'Gawd damn yuh, Surgeon Hume!'

Sabin walked to the sick man. He prepared wet applications for the rose flush. In the next cot, Jim Foster was breathing harshly. Sabin looked over his shoulder at Hume.

'Foster's in relapse,' he called.

Hume got up. 'We'll blister,' he said.

Together they treated the typhus case by blistering the length of the spine with ammonia and mustard. Hume wiped his hands and sighed. 'You might have made a good doctor, Sabin.'

'I might have made a lot of things.'

'I know. But it's a pity. As a doctor you would understand that men are men, regardless of whether they wear blue or gray. Political issues aside—oh, the devil with it.' He smiled and produced two fresh cigars. 'Have one, Sabin. One of Major Donaldson's supers.'

18

'Yankee weeds,' Sabin growled, and then his head snapped up as he heard loud voices in the barracks. Wood splintered. A man screamed thinly. Warner Giddings appeared at the door.

'Cap'n Shay, suh!' he yelled. 'Matt Duggan is a-killin' Phin Harris!'

★   ★   ★

Sabin burst through the doorway into the barracks. Matt Duggan stood in a corner holding the shattered leg of a table in one huge freckled paw. Now and then he stabbed the splintered end at the ring of faces which tried to close in on him. Behind him, Phin Harris was crouching in the corner, with his thin arms protecting his head. Blood dripped from his face.

'Get back, you bastards!' Duggan yelled. 'I'll fix this Galvanized Yankee.' He swung the table leg and stabbed viciously at the cowering little man behind him. He twisted his free hand into the loose folds of Harris' huck shirt and dragged him to his feet, stabbing at him with the club. The little man's left nostril was ripped raggedly up to the bridge of his nose. His lips were a bruised mass. His left eye was closing, swollen and bloody.

Sabin shoved a trooper aside. 'Get out of that corner,' he told Duggan.

Duggan whirled like a great cat, driving Harris back against the wall with his rump. Harris went down and Duggan trampled him with his big shoes. 'This stinkin' little bastard took the oath!' Duggan roared.

Sabin reached for the club. Duggan grinned and swung. The club lashed down on Sabin's left forearm. The club rose again and skinned the left side of Sabin's head.

'Bastard—bastard—bastard!' Duggan chanted.

Sabin reeled back, bumping into Lockerby. Lockerby jumped in front of Sabin, took a smashing blow on the head and went down. The rest of the men scattered away from the yelling giant.

Sabin pushed in. He danced back and forth, avoiding the swift blows, his breath thick in his throat. He dashed the blood from his left eye. He was out of condition. They all were with the exception of Matt Duggan who seemed to have the terrible vitality of a grizzly in his huge stinking body. Harris tried to crawl for cover but Duggan battered at his rib cage with his feet. Sabin timed a blow. He managed to paste Duggan's lips and teeth together in a bloody mass but his knuckles were cruelly ripped by the stained teeth.

Duggan spat blood and moved in on Sabin with the terrible set smile of the mentally unbalanced. Sabin hooked a left to the belly and brought his head up beneath the blocky chin. Duggan's mouth snapped shut. A wild blow of the club sent Sabin to his knees. He rammed his head into Duggan's groin, wrapped his long arms about the thick legs and up-ended the big man. Duggan's head smashed against the wall, rattling the whole flimsy building. He went down. Sabin got to his feet and smashed home a boot to the jaw to make sure the giant stayed down.

'Jesus,' Warner Giddings said. 'What a bloody fracas.'

Sabin swayed to the nearest window, thrust his head out and spewed a sour mess on the bare earth.

'The guards!' Kester said.

Sergeant Schmidt came into the barracks, followed by a file of Kansas militia with bayonets fixed on their Springfields. 'Godt damndt Rebels!' Schmidt yelled. 'Killing each odder! Maybe it iss goodt!'

Fraser threw a chair at the big German. One of the militiamen, his thin face drawn with fright, lunged at Fraser. Kester parried the thrust with his arm, throwing the soldier off balance. The needle bayonet rammed into the wall. Fraser snatched up another chair and swung it. Sabin closed in on him and smashed him to the floor with an uppercut.

Then, suddenly, it was all over. Four men lay in their blood on the dusty floor. The militiaman yanked his bayonet from the wall. Schmidt drew his big issue Colt from his

21

holster and cocked it. The clicking of the hammer sounded loud in the sudden quiet.

Schmidt looked from one face to the other. 'What iss?' he asked.

Kester wiped the sweat from his face. 'Harris came for his things. Duggan somehow knew he'd taken the oath. He went after Harris. The rest of us tried to break it up. Harris mighta been killed.'

'One less Johnny Reb,' said a militiaman.

'Shudt up, you!' Schmidt barked. 'You ain'dt as goodt a soldier as some of these men. Gedt that Harris and that Duggan to the hospital yedt.'

Sabin wiped the blood from his face and walked outside. Schmidt came up behind him. 'You'd better have Harris taken to the regular post hospital,' Sabin said.

'For why?'

'He's one of you now,' Sabin said quietly.

The pale eyes of the German held Sabin's. 'Yess. You are hurdt too.'

'I'll be all right.'

'Take that Harris to the dispensary!' the sergeant called. He tapped Sabin on the chest. 'You tell dese men to take it easy yedt. Next time maybe somebody shoodt. Dese militiamen is nervous. They don'dt like Rebels. They think you are wildt animals.'

'Dirty Dutchman,' said someone in the background.

The burly German ignored the remark. He

22

strode toward the gate followed by the shambling militiamen.

Sabin dabbed at the blood on his face. 'Schmidt is all right. He's a Regular. I think it gripes him to be in charge of the stockade and those strawfoot militia.'

Sabin walked to the hospital. Hume was working over the unconscious Duggan. 'I hear he might have killed you,' he said over his shoulder.

'Damned Yankee fools—letting Harris come back into the stockade.'

Hume jerked a thumb toward a chair. 'Sit down and take it easy. You'll need a few stitches.'

Sabin sat down wearily. He wondered how long he would be able to stand the gaff. Maybe he could make a break himself. Yet he didn't want to leave his men. Besides, there was Frank Khuyper to deal with. He had kept Miles in a cold stone cell in the guardhouse when the kid was still weak from his wound because Miles, in his sickness, had broken some minor prison infraction.

Hume finished with Duggan and set to work on Sabin. Afterwards he washed his hands in the blood-tinted water of a basin. 'Lie down for a while,' he said.

Sabin dropped on a spare cot and looked up at the sagging ceiling. His head throbbed and his lacerated knuckles stung like fire. There was little hope for his men being paroled or exchanged. Khuyper claimed they were little more than guerillas. The bloody memories of Quantrill and his raiders were still fresh on the war pages of the history of Kansas. The shifting border line between the Confederacy and the United States in that area was infested with Jayhawkers, wild Indians, deserters and conscription dodgers, and both Federal and Confederate governments had given short shrift to any men who were not part of recognized military units.

It looked as though Shay's Company would rot at Fort MacNaughton, eating half-raw food and dying of disease. As though to mock Sabin, the westerly wind crept into the sour-smelling room and teased him with its freshness.

He dropped off into a restless sleep.

CHAPTER FOUR

It was full dark when he left the hospital. He walked to the water trough and bathed his face. Someone approached through the darkness. He turned and saw Sergeant Schmidt.

'Shay,' the non-com said, 'you are wanted at headtquarters yedt.'

'Why?'

'You will find oudt. It iss nodt Captain Khuyper who wishes to see you. It iss Major Donaldson.'

Sabin wiped his face on his shirttail. 'More trouble?'

Schmidt just grunted.

Sabin walked with the big German to the gate. They passed through it and crossed the gully bridge to the parade ground of the fort. Somewhere a trooper was singing. The odor of fresh bread hung about the post, awakening hunger anew in Sabin.

Schmidt stopped in front of headquarters. The window light reflected from his polished buttons and the crossed sabers on his forage cap. 'There hass been hard fighting at Petersburg,' he said.

'So?'

'General Lee cannot escape.'

'Why are you telling me this, Schmidt?'

The German shrugged. 'The war will soon be over. General Sherman hass marched from Atlanta to Savannah midt sixty thousand men. Savannah iss now a base for the Union.'

There was a cold feeling in Sabin, not brought on by the searching wind which penetrated his thin clothing. He had heard that Lincoln had called out 300,000 more men. It was said that the Union had almost a million and a half men in uniform.

Schmidt jerked his thumb at the stockade. 'It is nodt goodt to see men penned up like animals. Soon I go west on the Oregon Trail. I wass hoping that you and your men would be free by then.'

'Thanks, Schmidt.'

Schmidt waved a beefy hand. 'Come. The major iss waiting.'

Schmidt ushered Sabin into headquarters and into an office. Sabin's hands closed into fists. Frank Khuyper stood by the window, immaculate in a fine broadcloth uniform. His long blond hair had been carefully brushed to bring out the deep wave in it. There was a cold handsomeness about the sonofabitch. Even Sabin had to admit it. The man's uniform fitted perfectly, emphasizing the breadth of his shoulders and the leanness of his waist. The thin line of his white collar accentuated the faint ruddiness of his skin against the blue of his dress blouse. The thought came to Sabin that here was a man who fancied himself a real stud.

Major Donaldson coughed. Sabin jerked his gaze away from Frank Khuyper and found himself looking into a pair of cool, steady gray eyes. Donaldson was chunkily built, with a fringe of curling burnsides framing a square, stern face that fairly shouted 'Regular.' Sabin took him to be a real man and a first class soldier.

'Wait outside, Schmidt,' said Donaldson.

Khuyper shifted his gaze from a roller map and eyed Sabin. Donaldson indicated a chair with a jerk of his thumb.

'Sit down, Captain Shay.'

'The man is a guerilla, sir,' Khuyper said in his smooth voice. 'I haven't seen fit to use his assumed rank.'

Donaldson shrugged. 'We have no sure knowledge that he *isn't* a Confederate officer. Until we know for sure, Khuyper, we can afford him the courtesy of his rank.'

A faint flush tinted the fine skin of Captain Frank Khuyper.

Donaldson leaned back in his chair. 'I hear there was quite a fracas in your barracks, Shay.'

'It was a damned fool thing to let Harris come back there after taking the oath,' Sabin said shortly.

Donaldson glanced at Khuyper. Khuyper turned his head slightly. Donaldson smiled.

'Why did you surrender as an enlisted man, Captain Shay?'

'I wanted to share the fate of my company. My brother was seriously wounded. I couldn't very well leave him to the tender mercies of a Yankee prison.'

'Humm. Well, there is no news on your exchange or parole, captain.'

'We're entitled to it, major.'

'Our government has changed its policy,' Donaldson said.

'Why?'

'Simple enough. The South is outnumbered. We can afford to leave our men in Rebel prisons. The South can't spare the men in Federal prisons. The Confederacy is being bled white of manpower.'

'They'll last.'

'No. The desertion list in the Confederacy is unbelievably high.'

Donaldson hooked an arm over the back of his chair. 'We have no proof that your company was a part of the regularly constituted forces of the Confederacy.'

'We are part of the Northern Military Sub-District of Texas, Brigadier-General Henry E. McCulloch commanding.'

'You have been listed as guerillas.'

'A lie thought up by Captain Khuyper.'

Donaldson's eyes were icy. 'Take care in what you say!'

'I accuse him of destroying company records which would have proved our status,' Sabin said.

Khuyper laughed. 'You have no right to accuse anyone of anything. The only difference between you and Quantrill is that he at least had the honesty to ride under the Black Flag.'

Donaldson slapped a hand down on the desk. 'Dammit! I've had enough of this quibbling!'

'Then get to the point,' Sabin said, 'or let me go back to my men.'

'Don't try me, Shay! I've had enough from

you arrogant Rebels.' Donaldson controlled his temper. 'Captain Hume will take the oath of allegiance tomorrow for service along the Oregon Trail.'

'Interesting,' Sabin said with cold politeness.

'Hume thinks a great deal of you, Shay. He has told me of your knowledge of the Plains Country. You were out there from '54 through '59?'

'Yes.'

Donaldson lit a cigar, eyeing Sabin keenly over the flare of the lucifer. 'Were you in the Army?'

'No. I scouted for Sumner in '57 against the Cheyennes between the Platte and the Arkansas. Later I served in the Utah campaign of '58.'

'You know the Sioux then?'

'The Otchenti Chakowin; the Seven Council Fires.'

Donaldson's eyebrows went up. 'You speak their tongue?'

Sabin shrugged. 'Enough to get by, with plenty of sign language to help out. I also speak a little Cheyenne and some Pawnee.'

'I see. Things are rough along the Oregon Trail. Seven hundred miles from Westport Landing to Fort Laramie, with one and a half graves figured for every one of those miles.'

'It never was a pleasure jaunt.'

'The Sioux and Cheyenne are as thick as

29

buffalo gnats along the Trail. The Arapahoes are doing bloody work west of Fort Laramie.'

Sabin grinned. 'You're said to have a million and a half men in your army. You should be able to hold the Indians in check.'

Donaldson turned to the map behind him. 'Before the war we had regulars out there. Tough in the prat. Disciplined. The hostiles respected them.'

'So?'

'Now all we have out there are volunteers. Their discipline is not of the best. Most of them are guarding the roads and the telegraph line from South Pass to Julesburg. But we need experienced Indian fighters.'

'I hope you get them.'

Donaldson flushed. He was used to respect, and he wasn't getting much of it from Sabin Shay. 'We expect bloody trouble on the Trail. The Indians know we're in a life and death struggle with the Confederacy. There has been hell to pay in Colorado. Last fall, Major Chivington of the Colorado Volunteers struck the Cheyennes under Black Kettle at Sand Creek. It was a hideous slaughter of innocents.'

'Get to the point, Donaldson.'

Donaldson frowned. 'I want you and your men to take the oath of allegiance to the United States for service along the Oregon Trail.'

'*Wa nee chee*,' Sabin said. 'No!'

30

'You have the word of the government that you will not be forced to fight against the Confederacy. Hume and Harris have already taken the oath.'

'Hume is a British subject. Harris is nothing more than a damned clay-eater.'

'Your brother is dead. Most of the men of your old company are dead or will die of disease before the end of the war.'

'We can thank Captain Khuyper for that!'

There was a silence.

'Yes,' Khuyper said thinly. 'I wish to God you were *all* dead.'

Donaldson waved a hand. 'Please leave the room, Captain Khuyper.'

The handsome officer closed the door behind him. Sabin looked steadily at Donaldson. 'That sonofabitch deliberately caused the death of many of my men, including my own brother.'

'So? I understand your men were in poor physical condition when they came here.'

Sabin leaned forward. 'Did Khuyper tell you he marched us here on foot from the Badwater on half rations?'

Donaldson's teeth closed hard on his cigar. 'I don't suppose you've heard of Andersonville prison in Georgia?'

'A little,' Sabin said.

Donaldson raised his voice. 'A filthy pesthole where over ten thousand Federal soldiers died in indescribable filth!'

31

Sabin hesitated. In a minute they would be shouting at each other. This was getting neither of them anywhere.

'You're an officer,' Donaldson said more temperately. 'We need you to influence your men to serve on the frontier. Sound them out. Ask them to take the oath. Within a week we'll have them on the way west, mounted on good horses, with the clean wind to blow the prison stench from their nostrils.'

Sabin shook his head. 'Call my guard,' he said.

Donaldson placed a sheet of paper in front of him. 'Read that—and *think* about it.'

Sabin read the paper and turned white.

'Yes,' Donaldson said. 'By order of the commanding general, Department of the Missouri, you and your men will either take the oath or stand court-martial as guerillas. You have no records to prove your existence as a Confederate unit. Quantrill has set a bloody precedent for you.' Donaldson's blocky face lost just a bit of its granite sternness. He tugged at his sideburns and coughed as if embarrassed. 'Captain Shay,' he said, 'I'm afraid that unless you take the oath, Frank Khuyper will have his pleasure. Because if you are found guilty of being guerillas, the only fate you can expect is the firing squad—every last man of you.'

Cold sweat ran down Sabin's sides in rivulets. He sat absolutely still and watched

Donaldson take a letter from the top drawer of his desk.

'I met a Colonel Bascomb, his son, and his daughter Marianne in Westport Landing,' the major said. 'Miss Bascomb heard I was traveling here. She asked me to give you this letter.'

Sabin took the letter. The faint odor of jasmine rose from it. He watched Donaldson stand up.

'The Bascombs are traveling west along the Oregon Trail to make a new home in Oregon,' Donaldson said.

Sabin stared at the letter. The last one he had received from her had come from New Orleans just before he left San Antonio for the Pease River. She had mentioned nothing then of traveling west, but only that she was sick of the domineering Yankees who had occupied the city since May of 1862.

★   ★   ★

Hamish Hume was asleep on a hospital cot. Sabin sat down at the surgeon's desk and split open the letter.

Westport Landing, Missouri
February 25, 1865

Dearest Sabin:

I have received no mail from you since you left San Antonio for frontier service. The news of your capture came to us from a paroled prisoner. We send our best wishes to you and Miles before we leave on our great adventure—for we are embarking on the Trail to Oregon! Father is arranging for our wagons and supplies for the long journey. We will soon leave for Fort Laramie. I am thrilled at the prospect of seeing wild Indians and the vast open spaces of the Plains.

My brother Stacy, poor boy, is with us. Stacy received his parole at New Orleans in the late summer of 1862, in case you did not know. The poor boy became quite ill of fever while held in a Federal prison. Of course it was difficult for Father to get permission to leave New Orleans and come north to Westport Landing, but as you know, he had *great* political influence in Washington before the war, and his old friends did not forget Colonel Clay Bascomb! He managed to find a way, the old dear, just as he *always* does.

We are looking forward to a fresh start in Oregon and Father has plans for a great manor there where I can be the lady of the house. He says the future of this country is in the West. I must close now, as a seamstress has come to fit me out with some traveling costumes. Is there no way you can be paroled or exchanged? You always loved the Great West, and I know that Oregon would be the place for you to settle down and make the mark in the world of which you are capable.

Need I say more, Sabin?

Take care of yourself and remember your old friends from the Crescent City. Perhaps we will see you again...

With Love,
Marianne

Sabin felt cold now, and not just because the sweat had dried on his body. Old Colonel Bascomb knew which side his johnnycake was buttered on. Getting out of the South while the getting was good, eh? It was like the old bastard to grease his way out of a mess and turn up smelling like a magnolia. Sabin was willing to bet he had most of his wealth with him, too. He had given Sabin a hard time before the war, demanding to know what plans he had for a future if he figured on marrying Marianne. Stacy had swaggered around in his gaudy militia uniform, lording it over Sabin, although Stacy had joined a home guard outfit which was not required to serve outside the state. That was 'poor' Stacy all over. He had sure learned from his dad.

But Marianne...

Sabin leaned back in his chair, thinking of her. The great blue eyes and the honey-colored hair. The smooth lips and skin. The full breasts and long legs. Marianne had held nothing back from him; there was a hot flame beneath that glacial beauty. Many times he had seen her oval face smiling in the embers of bivouac fires. Too many times. It wasn't good for a man in the field, and Lord knows it wasn't good for him now, in prison.

He sighed and glanced at Hamish Hume. Still asleep. He got up and went to a cabinet and took out a large bottle. It was labeled Poison. He had seen Hamish Hume label it. He sniffed it, then poured some of the 'poison' into a tincup. He sipped and smacked his lips.

Bourbon, he thought. Compliments of Major Donaldson, probably, like his goddam cigars.

Outside, the wind seemed to whisper from the dark reaches of the West. From west Kansas, Nebraska, Wyoming, Utah and far Oregon. It spoke softly of the muddy Platte, the Sweetwater, the Big Shandy, the Snake and the Umatilla. It hinted at roast buffalo hump broiled on the embers, and of the Shining Mountains and the Big Country. But most of all it brought to Sabin Shay the faint, clinging odor of jasmine.

CHAPTER FIVE

In the slow days which followed, Sherman won through to Savannah, and Lee was penned in Petersburg.

And here in this grim Yankee prison Big

Driver Ellis wasted and died. His huge body and tremendous strength had been no match for the rosy filth of erysipelas and the fatal blow of blood poisoning. Jim Foster put up a good fight against typhus, living through the chills and fever, the racking pains and prostrations, the purple rash, only to succumb at last to pneumonia. Jim left a wife and five kids on the banks of the Nueces.

Hamish Hume had left the stockade to wear Federal blue. Ellis and Foster joined the line of mounded graves. Matt Duggan returned to the barracks, silent and morose, keeping to himself, half insane with hatred. But it was gaunt Norton Fraser who argued against any plan of release other than that of a clean break from the stockade. The tough Texican could see only one way out, and half a dozen hotheads backed his wild idea.

Fraser's chance came when an epidemic of intestinal trouble hit the regular garrison and prisoners from the stockade were needed to carry on some of the fatigue details of the post. Fraser and his six conspirators volunteered en masse one afternoon to unload supply wagons which had just rolled in from Fort Leavenworth, and Sabin Shay volunteered with them. The eight ragged Rebels marched to the quartermaster wagon yard under the guard of four militiamen.

Fraser worked next to Sabin, carrying boxes from the wagon into the warehouse.

'Now don't get any ideas of stoppin' us,' he said in a low voice.

Sabin jerked his head. 'You damned fool. If you make a mistake like this it will be your last.'

They placed the box on a pile. Fraser wiped the sweat from his face. 'I'm sorry yuh volunteered with us,' he said. 'Me and the boys has it all figgered out. My advice to you is to get sick and go back to the stockade. Yuh try to stop us, Cap'n Shay, and you'll get hurt.'

Dusk came slowly, forming shadows. Here and there in the fort yellow lamplight held back the darkness. A corporal rounded a building. 'All right, Rebs! Back to the hawg pen! Quick march there!'

The prisoners obediently fell in and slogged toward the stockade. Sabin marched behind Fraser and ahead of Morton. The stockade gate creaked open. The corporal of the guard was just ahead of Fraser, in a hurry to get rid of his charges and take off for the mess hall. Fraser shot a glance at Sabin. Sabin shook his head. Fraser spat. Then he jumped directly behind the corporal like a great lean cat. Sabin ran forward but one of the prisoners thrust a foot between his driving legs. He hit the ground hard, bruising his face.

Norton whirled the corporal around and smashed a blow home to the jaw. He jerked the Springfield from the nerveless hands as the non-com went down. The prisoners moved silently and swiftly. Two to a man. One of the guards on the catwalk stared at the struggling men and then discharged his piece into the air, awakening echoes among the low bluffs across the Smoky Hill. He rammed home another cartridge, cocked and capped his piece and discharged both slug and ramrod down at the men below. The heavy slug struck Palley in the chest. The ramrod pierced his throat and stuck, equal lengths quivering before and behind. He went down with a grunt.

Sabin rolled from under the mass of stamping, thrusting feet. Three of the guards were down. Sam Farber staggered from the fight and collapsed against the stockade wall, gripping a smashed shoulder. Fraser broke loose, followed by MacGinnis, DeVries, Danby and Lewis.

Men yelled through the darkness. Feet thudded on the hard earth. The guard came up on the double. Fraser fired directly over Sabin's head, blinding him with the flash and heavy smoke. He crawled to one side, rubbing at his eyes. From somewhere he heard the impact of the bullet like a stick being whipped into thick mud and the coughing grunt of a man hard hit. The roaring voice of Sergeant Schmidt broke through the din, flailing his men into effective action.

Rifles spat steadily and Sabin's eyes cleared until he could see. Smoke drifted between the buildings. Sabin stood up beside a low building. A tall man raced across the parade ground with a stubby carbine in his hands. It was Captain Khuyper. Danby snapped a shot at him. Khuyper raised his carbine as though on the range. He fired. Danby went down as though pole-axed. The four remaining escapees ran for the corrals. But they hadn't figured on Frank Khuyper. He fired again. DeVries skidded face downward along the ground.'

'Oh God!' Lewis yelled. 'He's got one of them Yankee repeaters yuh load in the mornin' and shoot all day!'

Those were the last words Lewis spoke on earth. A slug drilled him through the head. Schmidt led his men behind a building and opened a flanking fire. MacGinnis threw down his rifle. Fraser sprinted for the corrals. A volley spoke from the militia rifles and the tough Texan jerked as the .58 caliber slugs riddled him.

Khuyper saw Sabin's movement. He snapped a shot at him. Sabin winced as a splinter ripped the skin of his left arm. Khuyper stalked toward MacGinnis. MacGinnis looked desperately over his shoulder. He held up his dirty hands. Khuyper fired deliberately from the hip. The soft slug plowed into MacGinnis' belly. He

40

doubled forward. The Spencer rapped twice more. MacGinnis' head smashed like a dropped egg.

Sabin Shay ran forward. Khuyper stood there in the wreathing smoke like a man in a dream and began to feed cartridges into the butt gate of the Spencer. Schmidt's detail doubled up through the smoke and slammed the big gate shut. Khuyper looked up and saw Sabin. He raised the carbine. Sabin gripped the hot barrel with his left hand and drove a fist against the officer's jaw, jerking the carbine free as Khuyper went down.

Something hard jammed into the middle of Sabin's back. 'Drop that Spencer,' a voice rasped behind him. He dropped the repeater.

Khuyper shook his head and wiped the blood from his mouth. 'You'll swing for this, you Rebel bastard.'

Major Donaldson came across the parade ground. Behind him the companies were forming under the whiplash of non-com's voices. Lantern light gleamed on bayonets.

Donaldson stopped in front of Sabin. 'Did you know about this break, Shay?'

'I heard rumors.'

'Why didn't you try to stop it?'

Sabin smiled coldly. 'I have no authority here. Besides—have you ever tried to reason with an angry Texan?'

'There will be hell to pay for this.'

Sabin looked past the officer at Khuyper.

41

'Yes,' he said, 'there *will* be hell to pay.'

Donaldson rammed a fist into his other palm. 'Damn it, have you made up your mind about taking the oath?'

Sabin looked at the bloody bundles which had once been his men. Khuyper, in his cold hatred, would make the rest of his company pay in blood.

'Give me until reveille tomorrow,' he said. 'You'll have my answer then.'

CHAPTER SIX

It was a silent group that clustered around Sabin's bunk after a tasteless mess. Seven men lay outside on the cold ground, covered with their ragged blankets. Five of them had been killed outright. Farber and Danby had died of their wounds. Sabin looked the survivors over grimly. Hard-pratted Texans for the most part, with a leavening of men from Arkansas, Tennessee and Missouri who had gone to Texas before the war. Men from the banks of the Brazos, Trinity and Colorado.

'You saw what happened this evening,' Sabin said.

'It was a good try,' Todd Shafter said.

'Mebee yuh should'a gone with 'em,' Al Carroll said. 'Fraser was loco to try.'

42

Sabin held up a hand. 'We've lost most of the company since the days on the Pease. Our chances for exchange couldn't be worse. We'll sit here and rot with Khuyper goading us until this company won't even be a whore's memory in San Antone.'

'So what do we do?' Duggan sneered. 'Write to that railsplittin' gorilla Lincoln?'

Sabin ignored him. 'You might as well know how the Confederacy stands. Lee is bottled up in Petersburg. Sherman has sixty thousand men in Savannah ready to go after Little Joe Johnston. The South is bled white.'

Sabin looked through the window. The wind seemed to be calling again. 'West of here, clear to the Pacific, there is land for the taking.'

'Ain't much takin' we can do,' Blalock Lott growled. 'Penned in the lion's den as Daniel was.'

'Them lions didn't chaw on him did they?' Warner Giddings asked.

'Maybe they didn't have a Khuyper amongst them,' Ames Lockerby said.

Kester took the bull by the horns. 'If you'll shut up and listen, you'll learn somethin'. The only way we can get outa here is by takin' the oath.' He stood up before anyone else had a chance to speak. 'Now I know what you're thinkin'. You're goin' round and round, talkin' about damn fool escape tries like Fraser did. Now listen to the captain

43

here.'

There was a pregnant silence in the drafty room.

'Major Donaldson has authority to recruit us into U.S. service,' Sabin said quietly. 'We can be out of here in a matter of days, headed west, with good horses and guns, and with supplies for the taking. There's a helluva lot of country out there. I know. I've been out there and so have some of you.'

'I ain't listenin' to no treason,' Chase Corby said. 'Even from *you*, Cap'n Shay!'

'Hear him out,' Kester said. 'We're all in this calabozo together. None of you thick-skulls has figured out a way. Now listen to a man as has.'

This was the crucial point. One wrong word and the scales would tip down against Sabin. Most of these men were like quicksilver on a platter, running every which way. Quick loyalties and quicker hatreds. Yet they said nothing as they sat in their rags eyeing Sabin.

Sabin stood up and paced back and forth. 'Let's face the truth. We're dying like flies here from disease. You saw what happened to Fraser and his hotheads. One more loco break like that and Khuyper will have a blood fiesta. There's nothing here for us but disease and death. Out on the Oregon Trail, with good horses and equipment, we'll at least have a chance to live. In a blue uniform, yes, but we'll be *men* again, not prison sheep!'

Warner Giddings heaved a sigh. 'I allus wanted to see the Oregon Trail,' he said, 'but I sure never wanted to see it dressed in Yankee blue.'

Cobb Howell, the tallest man in the company stood up. 'I'm fer it. Damned if I want to die like Driver Ellis or get gunshot by Khuyper. And when the time comes out there, Gawd help any bluebellies as gits in my way!'

Matt Duggan touched his scarred face and looked coldly at Sabin. 'I'm starvin' here. Nothin' to be gained by sittin' here like sheep ready for the slaughter. I'm fer it too.'

Sabin walked out into the starlit night and waited. After a while Kester came out and joined him.

'It's done,' Kester said. 'They'll all go.'

'*All* of them?'

'Who'd stay after what happened to Fraser and his boys?'

'I hope to God we're right.'

Kester laughed. 'No one leads those *ladinos* around by the nose.' He looked at the barracks. 'They all have two reasons. An inward one and an outward one.'

'What's yours, Charlie?'

'I've been doing a lot of thinking. I joined the Regulars in '46 and wore the blue until '61. Fifteen years is a long time to wear one uniform. I'm a professional. I guess it doesn't make much difference to me in the long run. The South can't win now. I'd have re-enlisted again after the war if the Federals would let me in.'

I wish my reason was as simple as that, Sabin thought.

'How about you, sir?'

Sabin shrugged. 'I think I'll turn in,' he said.

'Well—' Kester hesitated. 'Well, good night, sir.'

★   ★   ★

The oath-taking was over. Shay's Company had taken it like so many children swallowing a dose of sulphur and molasses, vile-tasting stuff but a necessary evil which cleans the bad humors of winter from the blood. And now, in the cold barracks, the converted Rebels eyed the pile of equipment which had been issued to them.

'Before Gawd,' Warner Giddings said as he surveyed the gear on his bunk, 'No wonder some of them Yankees fight so mean. After gittin' into all these fixin's a man's like to be mean enough to beat his own Granny with a stob of kindlin'.'

'You never had it so good,' a grinning Yankee said from the doorway.

Sharps New Model 1863, .52 caliber, cap-and-ball carbines with Maynard tape

46

primers were placed in racks. Pull throughs and other cleaning gear fell to the Texans. Colt Model 1851 caliber .36 cap-and-ball sixshooters had been issued along with sabers made by Ames of Chicopee, Massachusetts.

'What do yuh do with these?' Jonas Gilpin asked as he hefted the saber.

'Ride the redskins down with 'em,' Cob Howell said with a grin. 'At best they may be right handy to toast bread over a campfire.'

Warner Giddings, kid that he still was, got into his new regalia first. He looked down at the nine rows of yellow braid set horizontally across his chest. 'I have to be a trumpeter,' he said dolefully. 'Lookit the buttons. Forty-four of 'em!'

Kinston Forbes grinned. 'What with the sun shinin' on that and your horn,' he said, 'there ain't any Sioux between here and the Big Horns that won't set his sights on yuh, Warner. Yore positively outstandin', sonny.'

Sabin drew up the high-waisted trousers and put on the thick shell jacket. He held the forage cap, with its shiny brass saber ornament, in his hand for a few minutes, and then he put it on and looked in the mirror. He saw a lean face, with set gray eyes, staring at him from beneath the vizor. A curious uneasy feeling came over him.

Blalock Lott drew his pullthrough out of the barrel of his Sharps. 'I had my mind set on one of them load-in-the-morning-and-

47

shoot-all-day-Spencers like that bastard Khuyper has,' he said. 'But the Lord has provided and I accept with a glad heart.'

'That'll stop a Cheyenne,' Lockerby said as he worked his high collar together and hooked it.

'Cheyenne?' Lott said. 'How about a Yankee?'

Sabin turned. 'Enough of that talk,' he said.

Duggan pulled on his new boots. 'We don't take no orders from you, Shay,' he said. 'Private Shay, that is.'

The men looked at each other and then at Sabin. 'He's still company commander in my book,' said tall Cobb Howell.

'Go to hell,' Duggan said.

Howell eased back the hammer of his new Colt. 'One of these days, Duggan,' he said softly. *'One of these days.'*

Giddings buckled on his belt. 'How come they call us Galvanized Yankees?'

'When iron is galvanized,' Sabin said, 'it turns from blue to gray. Or the other way around. I forget.'

The men stood about inspecting each other in their thick blue shell jackets. To an outsider the hard-faced Texans were Union cavalrymen. But they carried a guidon of a different pattern in their hearts.

Ames Lockerby came into the barracks. 'I just heard somethin' interestin',' he said.

48

'Seems as though Captain Khuyper can't bear to part with us boys. He's been relieved of duty as post commander here and he'll be second-in-command under Donaldson.'

Nothing was said, but everyone in the room knew how everyone else felt. Howell's face cracked into a wide smile. 'Gawd,' he said, 'I feel my luck changin' already.'

Sabin sat down on his bunk and pressed his right hand down on the ticking. Inside the mattress was the guidon he had ripped from the bullet-splintered staff at the Badwater and carried beneath his shell jacket all the way to Fort MacNaughton. Two broad horizontal stripes, the upper white, the lower red, and a vertical blue stripe set against the staff, carrying on it the single white star of Texas. It was still stained with Miles' blood. Some day, somewhere, somehow, it would fly again in the breeze. He felt as sure of that as he was sure that Frank Khuyper did not have long to live.

CHAPTER SEVEN

The Oregon Trail stretched on either hand as far as the eye could see. Double sets of ruts forming a great roadway a hundred and more yards in width littered with filthy rags, broken bits of wood, smashed glass and decaying garbage. Dotting the barren earth were piles of manure: horse, ox, mule and human. The ceaseless wind blew the rags about, pinning them capriciously to clumps of brush or harrying them across the dusty flats. Floating high overhead, like a scrap of charred paper, a lone buzzard eyed the long line of blue clad soldiers who had halted at right angles to the Trail.

Sabin Shay held the bridle of his big bay. The bay kept jerking his hammer head. 'Take it easy,' Sabin said. The wind fluttered the arm-length cape of the greatcoat he wore, exposing the bright yellow lining. In the long days of travel from Fort MacNaughton the restlessness in him had somewhat abated. The column had crossed northwestern Kansas and the southwest tip of Nebraska. The South Platte was miles behind the column, and the North Platte was beyond the Trail, revealed by a low line of dusty trees.

Charlie Kester shook his canteen. 'Platte water,' he growled. 'You chew it instead of drink it.'

Warner Giddings grinned. 'Best way to drink that water,' he said, 'is to empty it outn' yore canteen and fill the canteen with forty-rod.'

'Some humorist,' Kester said sourly. 'How come every company has to have one, Cap'n Shay?'

Sabin shrugged. 'They're like saddle sores

and diarrhea, Charlie. They're issue.'

One hundred and fifty troopers waited, standing to horse, while in the distance a dozen troopers topped a rise and vanished from sight, scouting ahead. Major Donaldson was with them, leaving the troopers in the charge of Captain Frank Khuyper. Khuyper was studying a thin thread of dust or smoke which wavered up far beyond the rise.

'Injuns?' Aaron Fitch asked Sabin.

'*Quien sabe?* Emigrants maybe.'

'Helluva country.'

'Ain't no worse than some parts of Texas,' Giddings said.

'Yuh allus run off at the mouth like that?' Fitch demanded.

'Seven days a week,' Giddings said brightly.

'Six days shalt thou labor,' intoned Blalock Lott.

Sabin leaned against the big bay. The column was mixed. A few regulars, quite a few Kansas Volunteers, the rest Galvanized Yankees scattered throughout the squads. Miles behind them a battalion of Kansas Volunteer Infantry slogged through the dust, followed by the supply wagons. Sabin thoughtfully eyed the thin streamer which stained the bluish membrane of the sky. It was smoke. An emigrant campfire maybe. Or skulking Arapahoes or Pawnees.

A lone trooper rose above the ridge and

hammered down toward them, raising a thread of dust from the hard earth. The horse's hoofs drummed steadily. Then the trooper dipped out of sight as though the earth had swallowed him. Minutes later he surged up out of the hollow, galloped to Khuyper and circled his horse on the forehand, speaking swiftly and pointing toward the smoke. Sergeant Schmidt stood up in his stirrups. 'Shay!' he bellowed. 'On the double, you!'

Sabin mounted the bay and spurred it toward the officer, drawing rein beside Schmidt.

'Major Donaldson vants that you shouldt come to him yedt,' Schmidt said.

Khuyper's cold eyes studied Sabin. During the days on the trail, Sabin had felt those eyes on him constantly. Sabin nodded and spurred toward the trooper.

'Private Shay!' Khuyper said.

Sabin turned in the saddle.

'Haven't you learned how to soldier yet?'

Sabin saluted. Khuyper let him hold the salute and then slowly returned it. Sabin followed the Yankee trooper. The trooper grinned, revealing even white teeth. 'Bit of a rasper, isn't he?'

Sabin nodded.

The trooper looked back. 'I've served under plenty officers, good and bad, but there's something about that sonofabitch that gives me the crawls.'

'I know.'

'The name's Jim Lester.'

'Sabin Shay.'

'Pleased to meetcha,' Lester said. 'How do you like wearing blue?'

'It fits and it's warm.'

'Nice bunch of fellas, you Texicans.'

'We get by. What's doing up ahead?'

Lester shrugged. 'Donaldson found something. Sent for you. That's all I know.'

'Indians?'

'Yes.'

They rode down a long slope. Donaldson was on the far side of the hollow, lying on his belly in the dry grass, studying something with his fieldglasses. The scouts stood to horse in the hollow. The sun reflected from their scaled brass shoulder epaulets.

Sabin dismounted and handed the reins to Lester. He slogged up the slope in his stiff new boots. 'Sir,' he said to the major.

Donaldson moved. 'Lie down. Take these glasses. Look at that smoke.'

Sabin took the glasses and studied the smoke. It rose from the far side of a low knoll. 'Two wagons,' he said. 'One of them burning.'

'See any signs of life?'

'No, sir.'

Sabin began to sweep the slopes back and forth, until a slight movement caught his eyes. 'I've found something, sir.' He passed the glasses to the major. 'To the right of the wagons. Near that rise.'

'I'll be damned! A wolf!'

Sabin shook his head as Donaldson lowered the glasses. 'Wolf headdress worn by an Indian.'

'You've got abnormal vision.'

'Maybe I developed it out here to keep alive.'

'Arapahoe? Sioux? Cheyenne?'

'No. Pawnee.'

Donaldson looked relieved, 'Good! They're our friends. Good scouts. Hate the Sioux and Cheyenne like poison.'

Sabin took the glasses. 'Pawnees,' he said. 'Brainy, wide ranging, expert horse thieves as well as liars and extortioners. Loudmouths.'

'You know them that well?'

'Enough. I knew the Skidis better than the others. Stayed in a Kitkaha village once during a blizzard. They treated me fine and then followed me and stole two of my pack horses.'

'Some of them were enlisted as scouts last year under Captain McFadden.'

Sabin shrugged. 'I wouldn't consider them as allies.'

'They hate the Sioux and Cheyenne, as I said.'

Sabin smiled faintly at the officer. 'You're a little naive, begging your pardon, sir. They fight with you because they hate you less than the Sioux and Cheyenne.'

'What do you suggest?'

Sabin eased his collar. 'Ride over there and take a looksee. Best send a courier back to have the column brought up here. Don't let them graze their horses too far from the column, sir.'

'Thanks.' Donaldson slid down the hill and relayed the order.

Sabin and Donaldson rode west, followed by the scout detail. The smoke had thickened, and the wind raveled it out, bringing with it the odor of burning wood and leather, mingled with hot metal. There was a clinging, underlying odor, sickeningly sweet. Human flesh being cooked. Sabin knew it well.

Donaldson and Sabin put themselves ahead of the jangling troopers. Sabin glanced back at the bright brass shoulder epaulets on their shell jackets. They had rolled their greatcoats and fastened them to their cantle packs. 'Some sight,' he observed. 'The sun shining on those epaulets.'

'They're regulation,' Donaldson said.

'Where, sir? Against Jab Stuart? Mosby? Wheeler?'

Donaldson frowned. 'I see what you mean.'

'Remember, the Sioux don't use sabers, sir.'

Donaldson nodded. He studied Sabin.

'How do you feel?'

'Warm and well fed.'

'Is that all?'

'That's all, sir. Except that I'm damned curious about that smoke.'

Donaldson dismounted below a rise and walked up the slope. Sabin ran after him as he reached the skyline. He jerked at the major's belt and dragged him down. Just as he did so the boom of a heavy rifle sounded. A slug whispered inches above their heads.

Donaldson paled. 'Whew,' he said. 'That was a near thing. Thanks, Shay.'

Sabin crawled up behind a clump of grass and took off his forage cap with its bright brass insignia. He parted the grass and looked west. A rickety wagon was smoldering two hundred yards away. The axles had collapsed, dropping the bed to the ground. The osnaburg tilt was still smoldering. The traces had been cut and lay on the sloping ground like coiled snakes. Another wagon was fifty yards beyond the first. A wisp of powder smoke drifted away from it.

'Someone's still alive,' Donaldson said.

'Damned good shot too.'

Sabin studied the ground. Some cloth fluttered against a bush. A heap of cloth lay behind a clump of sage. He lay still, resting his chin on his hands.

'We'll go forward,' Donaldson said.

'No!'

'There are no Indians in sight.'

'That's the time to look for them, sir.'

Sabin took the glasses. The good German lens picked out every detail. The heap of clothing behind the bush was a dead man, more likely a boy. A charred mass clung to one of the rear wagon wheels. Sabin swallowed dryly. A man had been lashed to the wheel while the wagon roasted him in hot flame.

Sabin shifted the glasses. The wolf was gone. He handed the glasses back to the major. 'I think the Pawnees are gone, sir.'

Donaldson cased the glasses and jumped up. He waved his arms and hit the ground just as the rifle spat flame from the intact wagon. The slug keened overhead. Sabin grinned. He stood up and waved his cap and then ran fifty feet to one side, waved the cap again and then dropped as the rifle spoke for the third time. Then Sabin slowly rose erect and stood there. This time there was no shot.

'Let's go, sir,' he said.

They rode slowly toward the wagons. Sabin half-cocked his Sharps. The major held his issue Colt. One hundred feet from the wagons Sabin drew rein. 'United States Cavalry!' he called out. He glanced at the body behind the bush. He had been right. It was just a kid, no more than sixteen, with a bloody pipe ax buried in the back of his skull.

The osnaburg tilt moved a little. A slender

57

man came out, cradling a long-barreled Sharps in his arms. A wide-brimmed hat flopped over his face.

'Are you all right?' Donaldson asked.

The slim man came forward and grounded the rifle, lifting the hat brim from in front of the face.

'My God!' the major said.

'Amen,' Sabin said quietly.

It was a young woman, dusty of face and with powder-stained hands. 'Are you two alone?' she asked. 'There are about fifteen of them around here. Indians I mean.'

They dismounted. 'Look around, Shay,' the major said.

Sabin slid from the hammerhead bay and loosened his issue Colt in its holster. He glanced curiously at her as he walked past. Plain looking, with auburn hair tied up beneath her dusty hat. The eyes caught and held his attention. Almost too big for the oval face. Hazel ... reddened by trail dust. Her firm breasts pushed out against the thin huck shirt.

The rest of the scout detail rode up as Sabin ascended a rise. To the west was flat plain, stippled with Russian thistle and sagebrush. Dust raveled up from a ridge. Someone was driving horses at a fast clip. He saw no sign of life except the lonesome buzzard which had beat its way west against the steady wind, and now hung high overhead as though inhaling the odor of the feast it expected. Sabin went back down to the wagons.

The troopers had covered the boy with a blanket. Two of them were cutting the half-charred corpse from the wagon wheel. The young woman had removed the hat from the coiled helmet of her hair. Now and then the troopers glanced at her. One of them picked up a shovel lying beside the burning wagon.

'They were Pawnees,' she said in a monotone. 'Dad wasn't afraid of them. Some of them had been with the wagon train as scouts. They were friendly enough then. My father became ill. Too ill to move. The wagons went on without us. This morning we knew the Pawnees were watching us. My brother wanted to go on but Father had gotten worse. I rode ahead to get help. Then I heard the shooting. I rode back too late. The Pawnees were driving off the stock. Freddie was lying behind that bush. You saw my father. He was too sick to know what they intended, I guess. A few of them came back to get me. Then they saw your dust. They rode away.'

The shovel grated against the earth. A horse shied and blew, dancing away as the troopers carried the dead boy past him.

'Your name?' Major Donaldson asked.

'Katherine Williams. My father was Seb

59

Williams. We're from Pike County, Missouri. We were going to Oregon.' She bit her lip to hold back the bitter tears. 'Why did they leave us? Why?'

Sabin looked away. It was a helluva big country for two wagons, a woman, a boy and a sick man. Some bastard had gone on and left them.

Donaldson stripped off his gauntlets and slapped them against his left hand. 'I'll make a report on this.'

'It won't bring back the dead,' Katherine Williams said.

Donaldson flushed. 'Connelly!' he called out.

'Yes, sir!'

'Ride back to the column. Tell Captain Khuyper to bring them up. We'll bivouac here. Smartly now!'

Connelly galloped off, looking apprehensively at the brooding ridges.

Sabin unhooked his canteen and proffered it to the girl. 'You can wash a little with it if you like,' he said.

Her eyes held his. 'Thank you, sir.'

'The name is Shay. Sabin Shay.'

'Thank you, Sabin Shay.'

The sun died in a welter of rose and gold. Dust rose from the beating of hoofs as the column threaded its way down the far slope. The graves were almost done.

The girl appeared at the back of her wagon,

60

now wearing a threadbare but neat gingham dress. Trooper Lester whistled softly as he saw her. Sabin turned quickly. In a short time she had done wonders. Her hair had been uncoiled, brushed and re-coiled. A bonnet hung from its strings at the back of her neck. Sabin caught a flash of white stockings as she placed small feet on the ground. The dress seemed to have lifted up her young breasts.

She came to Sabin and handed him his canteen. 'I'm afraid I used it all,' she said.

'It's all right, ma'am.'

She did not look at the covered bodies, but watched the troopers ride toward the bivouac area.

'Who was the wagon master of the emigrant train?' Sabin asked.

'There really wasn't any.'

'So? It isn't wise to travel without some kind of organization.'

She closed her hands tightly. 'It was organized. We were delayed at Westport Landing when Father became ill. Our own train went on without us. We joined a private train which was going through to Fort Laramie. They had paid guards.'

'A private train?'

'Yes. Owned by one family. Nine wagons and a Dearborn. They had ten men as guards and a few Pawnees as scouts.'

A curious feeling came over Sabin. 'Whose

61

train was it?'

'Colonel Clay Bascomb's. He said they couldn't afford to wait for us. I think he thought Father had cholera. That wasn't so.'

Sabin's face darkened. He could almost see the imperious face of Colonel Bascomb with its immaculate goatee and curling mustachios. The smooth plump face and the ice-chip eyes of Marianne's father. It was like him, the self-centered sonofabitch.

A wolf howled far from the north. A moment later another answered it from the west, closer to the camp. Then a third one howled from the south. The Pawnees were out there, ringing the camp area. Waiting, waiting, waiting.

CHAPTER EIGHT

The bivouac fires had smoldered low, leaving a thick scarf of smoke hanging in the windless air. The prairie night was velvety soft, prophesying the slow oncoming march of spring. It was chilly away from the fires, and those men who had taken to their blankets lay muffled like mummies, heads resting on horse-stinking saddles, forage caps low on their noses. Now and then a fire flared up, revealing the eyes of the horses on the picket lines like moist jewels.

Sabin Shay sat huddled in his issue blanket, at the mess fire of his squad. The Yankees of the squad had gone to their blankets, leaving Sabin with Charlie Kester, big Cobb Howell and little Warner Giddings. Giddings slowly polished his spang new trumpet. There wasn't a windjammer in the column, footslogger or yellowdog, who could match Warner Giddings when he put spit into a horn.

The infantry fires were beyond the cavalry fires, close up under the knoll. The beetle crushers hadn't had much to say since they pulled in long after dark, furred with dust. A good many of them were Johnny Raws, marching on feet that had swollen, then blistered, then developed into a raw mass, all one with socks and shoes.

A lean figure picked its way between the sleeping men and stopped beside Sabin. He looked up into the face of Hamish Hume, now wearing first lieutenant's bars on his blouse. The green sash of the Medical Department circled the waist of his single-breasted frock coat. 'How does it go, Sabin Shay?' he asked.

'Set a spell,' Cobb Howell said. 'There's good Yank coffee in the pot, suh.'

Hume sat down on a saddle. 'I've been treating diarrhea, constipation, scalded feet, blisters and indigestion,' he said. 'Yankees are no different from Johnny Rebs, it seems.

In that respect anyway.'

The shrieking laugh of a coyote came out of the black velvet far beyond the fires.

Cobb Howell spat. 'Damn 'Pawnees,' he said. 'What they figger on doin' out there?'

'Snap up a stray horse,' Sabin said.

'You're sure they were Pawnees?' Hume asked as he filled a cup with bitter coffee.

Sabin nodded.

'Arapahoes raid around here, don't they?'

'Yes. Farther west as a rule.'

'Treacherous bastards,' Kester said.

Now they could hear the wolves far out, beyond the fire reflections, talking among themselves.

'Makes a man feel queerlike,' Kester mused, 'hearing them, knowin' they're humans like us.'

'Ain't nothin' crazier than a white man,' Giddings said as he adjusted the yellow worsted cord on his trumpet. 'Look at us. Fight like hell against the bluebellies—then we *jine* 'em. Yuh figger thet ain't loco?'

Howell spat into the fire. 'We got us a reason.'

'Shut up, Cobb!' Kester snapped.

Hamish Hume studied the quiet men with his sharp eyes. 'What's going on here?' he asked.

Sabin yawned. He wasn't sure where Hume stood in the matter of his new loyalty. 'I ever tell you hombres about the Pawnee Crazy

Dog Society?'

'Uh-uh,' Kester said swiftly. 'Tell us.'

Sabin grinned. 'They go out ahead of their battle line, stripped to the buff, with feathers hanging from their privates. They tie their privates to a rope and fasten the other end to a stake in the ground. By God, they'll stay there too, to fight, unless one of their friends cuts the rope.'

'Helluva A note if a friend got too excited and cut too close,' Kester said, 'Hawww!'

But Hume kept on watching Sabin. There was little Sabin could conceal from the canny Scot.

A trooper came to the fire. 'The major wants to see you, Shay. On the double!'

Sabin yawned. 'Double time yourself,' he said. He dropped his blanket and stood up behind Hume. He shook his head warningly at his three comrades and then placed his right hand over his mouth before he walked away.

Donaldson was seated on a carpet camp stool under the patched wagon tilt which served him as a tent. He returned Sabin's salute. 'I've been listening to those damned wolves out there,' he said.

'Pawnees, sir,' Sabin corrected.

'Same thing.' Donaldson peered intently at Sabin. 'I'm an old soldier, Shay. I can smell trouble in an organization long before it breaks.'

Sabin raised his head a little. 'Sir?'

'I don't like the way your Texans look at Captain Khuyper.'

Sabin grinned. 'I've seen a good many of your Yankees do the same thing, sir.'

Donaldson grunted angrily. 'Watch your tongue! There isn't much discipline in you or your men. I often wonder how you ever had any control over them at all.'

'They *love* me,' Sabin said dryly.

For a moment anger struggled for control of Donaldson's face and then he smiled. 'Touche!' he said. 'I had no business saying that, Shay.'

'Forget it, sir. You didn't ask me here to talk about Frank Khuyper.'

Donaldson drummed his fingers on his camp table. 'Things are easy now. But today we got a taste of what's in store for us. I've got to get this column through to Fort Laramie in good shape. But I haven't a really decent scout in the whole organization.' Donaldson paused. 'I'd like you to take over as my chief scout until we reach the fort.'

'Why, sir?'

'You know the Plains Indians. Surgeon Hume has told me quite a bit about your experiences with the Sioux.'

'Cheyennes, sir.'

'Same thing. Although I hear the Cheyenne women are considered the beauties of the plains.'

Sabin studied Donaldson. *How much had Hume talked?*

'What do you say, Shay?'

'I'm just a yellowleg trooper, major.'

'Then I must order you to take the detail. I had hoped you'd volunteer.'

Sabin smiled. 'You can order me to take it, sir. I'm too old a soldier to volunteer for anything.'

Donaldson glowered a little but made his peace. 'Fine. Report to me at dawn. You can pick your own men. Good night. Shay.'

'Good night, sir.'

'Shay!'

Sabin turned.

Donaldson shoved a box of cigars toward him on the table. 'Light up,' he said gruffly.

Sabin took a super. He nodded. 'Thanks, sir.'

Outside the tent, Sabin paused to light his smoke. He stood there in the darkness, remembering. He had lived with the Cheyenne for a time, in the winter of 1857–1858. He had been damned sick with fever and a Cheyenne girl had nursed him. He had been a long way from Texas, and young, and a hell of a lot more romantic than he was now. So he had drifted into living with her. Pretty Hands was her name, and she had been no more than sixteen when he married her. The Cheyennes in the sub-band of Little Eagle had accepted them as man and wife.

67

That is, all of them had except Standing Bear, son of a Sioux father and Cheyenne mother, who lived with his mother's clan amongst the Cheyennes. Standing Bear had wanted Pretty Hands. Sabin had taken her. Standing Bear had left to live with the Sioux where he was known as Mato Najin in their tongue.

Sabin had left Little Eagle's camp in the spring, planning fully and sincerely to return. That summer he met Marianne Bascomb, and Pretty Hands faded from his mind...

Sabin looked about the sleeping camp and then at the tent of the major. *How much did Donaldson know?*

The bivouac had quieted down. The only movements were the occasional stamping of a horse and the pacing of sentries. The supply wagons were neatly aligned, with Katherine Williams' wagon a few yards beyond the last one. Sabin threaded his way between sleeping men. A guard stepped out from behind the end supply wagon.

Sabin halted. 'How is she?' he asked softly.

The guard was a Yank infantryman. His hair was whitish gray beneath his forage cap. 'She's all right, Johnny.'

Sabin nodded. 'She's had a helluva time.'

The older man leaned on his Springfield. 'Yeh. The major picks me out to stand guard. Me and Jonas Scribner. Guess he figgers we're too damned old to be much interested.'

Sabin grinned.

'You goin' to smoke all of that seegar?'

'It's yours.'

'Thanks. I'll cut off the tip and chew the rest. Man can't smoke on guard but he sure as hell can chew.'

There was a faint movement in the brush beyond the wagon. Sabin handed the guard his cigar. 'Mind if I look around in the brush?'

'You got more guts than I have, Johnny. Not with them Pawnees prowlin' around, I don't. Go ahead—but one thing, Bub! Don't try to git into that waggin!'

Sabin drew his Colt and padded into the brush. He stopped fifty feet from the wagon to listen. The wolf howling had died away. Maybe they were in closer now, hoping to pick off a stray. Sabin waited. The guard drifted off behind the line of supply wagons, his jaws moving steadily. Minutes drifted past and then Sabin heard a faint scraping noise. He caught a furtive movement not fifteen feet away. Sabin reversed his Colt and held it by the long barrel. He bent his knees to lower himself.

Then he saw the dark outline of a man inching along on his belly. This was no Pawnee, slick with rancid grease, and with roached hair. The odor of sweat-soaked wool came to Sabin. The soldier raised himself to hands and knees and stared at the wagon, turning his head slowly from side to side like a questing bear. He did not see the tall grim man watching him. He stood up and padded toward the wagon with one hand outstretched to part the osnaburg.

Sabin moved fast. He thrust his Colt beneath his belt, gripped the soldier by his blouse, whirled him about and crashed a big fist against his jaw. There was no outcry. The man never knew what hit him.

Sabin crouched over the fallen prowler and looked about. There was no movement in the wagon. He dragged the man into the brush and squatted beside him, raising the head by the shaggy hair. He swore silently as he looked into the brutish face of Matt Duggan.

Sabin snapped out the blade of his caseknife. Methodically he cut through the thick leather belt and slashed the shell jacket here and there. He cut the laces of the heavy issue shoes and slashed the leather into ribbons. He inserted the point at the bottom of the trouser legs and ripped the heavy material all the way up to the knees. Then he carefully cut out the crown of the forage cap. He grinned as he contemplated the wreckage. Matt Duggan would have hell's own time with his non-coms and officers in the morning.

CHAPTER NINE

The long dusty column was climbing from the plains country into the plateau country, the transition marked by the curious spindle-shaped Chimney Rock which rose from a cone of talus rock.

'Seems to me I've seen one like that somewhere before,' Jim Lester mused as he rode beside Sabin and Cobb Howell.

Cobb Howell shifted his chew of spit-or-drown. 'Hells-fire, Yank,' he said, 'yuh never seen a woman with one like thet.'

Lester grinned. 'You ever been in Chicago, Reb?'

Sabin turned in his saddle. The point detachment of the column was a good two miles behind them, marked by a streamer of dust. They had traveled the Coasts of Nebraska at a steady pace, eating up the long miles. Somewhere back there was Katherine Williams.

As though reading Sabin's mind, the Yank trooper spoke up. 'Funny thing about that girl back there insisting on going on to Fort Laramie, all alone with that one rickety wagon.'

'Guess she had nowhere's else to go,' Howell said.

Sabin thought of the girl's answer to Major

71

Donaldson when he had mentioned the fact that Katherine could go back with the first military unit they met traveling east. 'No, major,' she had said quietly. 'Dad wanted to go to Oregon. It was all he had in his mind after he was discharged from the Army in '62. I'll go on. I can take care of myself.'

Sabin wondered if she had known about Duggan prowling about her wagon. Duggan was now tramping behind a wagon, his wrists lashed together, tied to the axle by a length of rope, eating dust. He would have gotten far worse punishment if his superiors had found out he had planned to molest the lone girl in the column.

There was little for Sabin and his detail to do except watch the distant smoke or dust threading up against the clear skies. Sabin had picked out some Yankees for his scouts, along with Cobb Howell, Ames Lockerby, Gus Feichter, Jesse Tinsley and Chase Corby. Donaldson had seen to it that the ex-Rebels were accompanied by Yanks three to one, with the exception of Sabin's personal detail.

Sabin had a feeling that they were riding in a huge bowl, with the dim rim peopled by hostiles. But the Indians wouldn't jump as strong a column of yellowlegs and walk-a-heaps such as the one now traveling west beneath their slitted eyes.

The days had been fairly mild for March. There was no haze as yet. Everything stood out clearly, deceptive as to distance.

'Hey!' Lester said. 'Look there!'

Sabin looked up. A lone horseman had appeared on a ridge ahead of them, outlined against the sky, as though etched there by a master hand. The pony was painted for war and his tail was tied up. The warrior wore a bonnet. The wind fluttered the many feathers. He sat there, less than half a mile away, watching the three scouts. Sabin drew rein and felt for his fieldglasses. He drew them out and focused them. The face of the warrior swam into view. It was eagle-like, the whole silhouette thrust out, saddle-leather in color. The nose was imperious and immense.

'Pawnee?' Lester asked in a curiously strained voice.

Sabin shook his head. 'The warbonnet should tell you that, Jim.'

'Cheyenne then?'

'No. He has the four-pointed sacred star on his shield cover. Arapahoe.'

Cobb Howell spat. The juice made a sound like that of a pack of playing cards dropped in the thick dust. 'They ain't such a much,' he said.

'Bad enough,' Sabin said. 'They don't give a damn for prestige. They like booty. Shifty bastards.'

'He friendly?' Lester asked.

'Not with a warbonnet on.'

'Maybe he's hunting.'

'On a white horse? No. Bad medicine for an Arapahoe.'

Lester eyed Sabin. 'Where'd you learn all this?'

'I lived with the Cheyennes for a time. The Arapahoes are allies of theirs. Curious though, they don't speak the same language, and don't intermarry. Good fighters, the Arapahoes, but not on a level with the Cheyenne and Sioux.'

The warrior raised a heavy musket. The weapon bellowed, driving a thick cloud of smoke ahead of it. The slug whipped past Jim Lester. 'The sonofabitch!' Lester said.

He set the steel to his dun. The big horse shot forward.

'Come back!' Sabin yelled.

Lester unsnapped his carbine from its sling and capped it at a dead run. The dun's hoofs drummed on the hard earth. The warrior slung his rifle and took his lance in hand. Lester came on, riding hard.

'What do we do?' Howell asked.

'Set tight. That red bastard ain't alone.'

'That figgers.'

Lester fired at a hundred yards. The warrior forestalled the trooper by turning his pony away and hanging over the far side. The slug went wild. Lester slung his carbine and ripped out his saber with a slither of steel, drawing his Colt with his left hand. The Arapahoe turned tail and vanished over the

74

ridge. Then Lester was atop it, eager saber extended. He too disappeared, leaving a wraith of dust to mark his passage.

Sabin dismounted. 'Get in that hollow, Cobb,' he said. 'Maybe you think we ought to back his play?'

'God no! He's a loco Yank, ain't he?'

They led the horses into the hollow and capped their Sharps. There was no sign of Lester. Then a rifle popped. It was followed by the snapping discharge of a Colt. Then silence.

Sabin dropped to the ground and slid his Sharps forward. Minutes drifted past. He looked back. The point was not in sight.

'There he is,' Howell said.

Sabin turned. The warbonneted warrior was back on the skyline, watching them. He shook his lance and then held up a dark scrap of something. Sabin fixed his glasses on the dark object. It was a dripping scalp. Some of the blood stained the white side of the horse. His guts boiled a little. He had liked Jim Lester. 'He's done, Cobb,' he said.

Cobb snapped up his rear sight and slid the movable sight slide upward to clear the V notch which was set at two hundred yards. 'I figger he's a lot closer than when we first saw him,' he said.

'Two hundred and fifty yards.'

'About thet.' Cobb settled himself. 'Wisht I had my old Hawken rifle my pappy give me

75

when I growed up.'

The Arapahoe sat there, evidently waiting for another sortie. Cobb had been the best shot by far in a company of better than average marksmen. He let out half of his breath and tightened his big hand on the small of the stock. The carbine barrel wavered, then settled. The big hammer snapped down. The carbine roared dully, driving smoke ahead of it. The Arapahoe moved. He was too late. The 475-grain slug smashed into his naked chest, driving him from the back of his pony. The pony buck-jumped and vanished over the ridge, dragging the corpse behind him. There was nothing left on the ridge but the warbonnet, its feathers fluttering in the wind.

Cobb shifted his chew and spat. 'These Beecher's Bibles ain't bad little guns,' he said. 'I didn't think I'd get him.'

'Look,' Sabin said.

The ridge had sprouted a score of warriors. The sun shone on greased hides and the brass trim of weapons.

'There they are,' Howell said as he reloaded. 'Salt, pepper, and gravel in the grease.'

Sabin squeezed off, parting the feathers of a warbonnet. Howell fired as Sabin reloaded. His bullet struck a paint pony. Sabin fired as Howell reloaded. Most of the warriors flowed down the far side of the ridge, leaving eight warriors who spread out in a crescent, circling down the ridge at far range.

Howell glanced back over his shoulder. 'Here comes the point,' he said. 'Burnin' leather.'

The dozen troopers pounded up heavily with a jangling of saber sheaths. Sabin looked up into the flushed face of Frank Khuyper. The Arapahoes cautiously withdrew, but stayed on the near side of the ridge.

'Where's Lester?' Khuyper asked as he wiped his face.

'Dead, sir.' Sabin stood up and reloaded.

'Dammit! Where?'

'Beyond the ridge, captain.'

'You let a few skulking Indians cut him off?'

Sabin capped the Sharps. 'There are a helluva lot of them beyond that ridge,' he said quietly.

'I see just eight!'

'I said there were more—*sir*.'

Khuyper turned in his saddle. 'Corporal Ames!'

The non-com kneed his horse close to the officer.

'Get back to the column. Tell the major we're going to teach some Cheyennes a lesson.'

'Arapahoes,' Howell said.

'Shut up!' Khuyper rasped.

Sabin frowned worriedly. He hated

Khuyper's guts but he had nothing personal against the sweating troopers. 'Stay put, sir. They won't attack.'

Khuyper checked the caps on his Colt. 'I can ride through a hundred of them with these men. The stinking scum!'

Faces were taut beneath forage cap vizors. The men looked nervously at each other and then at the ridge. The eight warriors sat there, speculating on what the Long Knives planned to do. Maybe the Long Knives would bite on the oldest dodge in Plains fighting. Set a trap and draw the soldiers into it. Then surround, circle in close and cut them down. It usually worked fine. It had failed with the scouts. Maybe there was still a chance.

Khuyper waved his pistol at Sabin. 'Mount!'

'The major ordered me to avoid contact, sir.'

'Dammit! I said "Mount!"'

Sabin grew tense as Khuyper aimed the Colt. 'I'm sorry, sir. I have my orders, sir.'

Howell moved a little. The hammer of his Sharps double-clicked back. The muzzle moved to cover Khuyper. Khuyper looked from one to the other of the two ex-Rebels. 'Sit there then, you yellow-bellied Rebel scum!'

Khuyper struck his spurs in deep. The big gray lurched forward. The troopers clattered on behind the impetuous officer. Sabin watched them as they plowed up the ridge, sabers extended, Colts held at the ready. The Arapahoes fired a few scattered shots and then spread out to both sides, lashing their ponies out of the way, and then over the ridge. Khuyper breasted the ridge, slowed down, and then waved his Solingen saber. The detachment vanished from sight.

A few seconds passed. Then shots crackled. Smoke drifted up.

Cobb Howell spat. 'Right smart doin's over there, Cap'n Shay.'

The dust was rising from the east where the main column hotfooted forward toward the sounds of shooting.

'Here they come,' Cobb said.

The troopers had reappeared, but not all of them. Khuyper was leading the way, stabbing home the steel. Seven men were behind him, riding as if the devil was on their heels and the fires of hell had been freshly stoked for them.

The troopers clattered to a dusty halt and slid from their saddles, jerking their carbines from their slings without orders. Khuyper sheathed his blade with a ring of steel. His breath was thick in his throat as he looked up the ridge.

'Damn fool,' a trooper said in a low voice to Sabin. 'There was forty of them Arapahoes over that ridge. In the draws. They come up

outa them like screeching devils and cut us to
ribbons. Kelly, Hansen, Finster, Ross and
Ollinger won't draw this month's pay. The
crazy glory hungry bastard!'

A single frenzied scream, cut off short,
drifted to them on the wind, and then there
was nothing but the rustling of the dry
bunchgrass and the stamping of the lathered
horses to break the silence.

The column came up in a veil of dust.
Donaldson drew in his gray. 'Well, Captain
Khuyper?'

Khuyper said, 'Arapahoes, sir. I tried to
cut them down. They outnumbered us. I lost
five men.'

Donaldson turned to Sabin. 'Didn't you
warn him?'

'I did, sir.'

Khuyper shot a look of feral hate at Sabin.
'The oldest dodge on the plains,'
Donaldson said. 'I saw it through my glasses.
Captain Khuyper, return to your company!'

Sabin watched Khuyper go, and loved it.
'Skulking Pawnees behind us,' Donaldson
growled. 'Arapahoes ahead of us. What next?'

Sabin swung up on his horse. 'Just the
Sioux and the Cheyennes, sir. Let me tell the
major that they'll raise more pure,
unadulterated hell than any Pawnees or
Arapahoes.'

Donaldson eyed the deserted ridge. 'Will
you scout ahead?'

'That's my job, sir.'

'Watch yourself.'

Sabin rode forward, followed by Howell. They ascended the ridge, dismounted, and wormed forward on their bellies. The Arapahoes had vanished. Dust rose from the north. But the warriors had left something for the troopers to meditate on. Sabin focused his glasses and then lowered them quickly.

He and Howell mounted, waved the column on, then rode down into the vale of death and mutilation. The Arapahoes had done their work thoroughly, with savage relish. Eyes had been gouged out and placed on rocks. Noses, ears and chins had been hacked off. Teeth were scattered about like bloody kernels of corn. The men had been gutted and their entrails dragged out. Hands and feet had been hacked from the bodies. Their privates had been severed and placed on the hacked faces. Ribs had been separated by slashing axes. Arrows stuck up like grisly growths from the softer parts of the bodies. There were punctured holes in every sensitive part of the corpses.

Donaldson spurred down beside the scouts. 'I'll divert the column,' he said thickly.

Sabin shook his head. 'March them past, sir. Let them see what the Plains Tribes do for vengeance.'

'Vengeance?'

'Have you forgotten Sand Creek, sir? I

heard there were many lodges of Arapahoes there.'

Donaldson nodded. 'Yes. You're right. The men will be marched past.'

The column, horse, foot and wagons, was led past the sprawling mess of bodies. Some of the younger soldiers spewed their bellies empty on the bloody grasses. Sabin waited until he saw the rickety wagon of Katherine Williams. He rode toward her and stopped beside it as she drew rein on the ridge.

'Turn here,' Sabin said quietly.

Her face was tired beneath the dust. 'Why?'

'There's been fighting.'

The horses shied at the thick odor of fresh blood in the air. Sabin tethered his horse to the tailgate and walked to the front of the wagon. 'Move over,' he said. 'I'll drive.'

She did not speak, but slid across the warped seat. Sabin touched up the team and drove it south, behind a low ridge. The wind hummed through the wires of the telegraph line and stirred the dust in the ruts of the Oregon Trail. Half a mile west Sabin could see where the telegraph line had been cut and dragged by horses. Two poles had been hacked down.

She wiped the dust from her face. 'I didn't thank you,' she said.

'For what, Miss Katherine?'

'For stopping that soldier from coming into

my wagon.'

'You saw—'

'Yes.' She touched her hair. 'I was all right. I had a loaded pepperbox pistol.'

He grinned. 'Sure you can take care of yourself, is that it?'

'I always have.'

'Why don't you go back? Haven't you relatives in Missouri?'

'No.'

'Friends?'

'Most of them are already in Oregon.'

He drew rein half a mile past the place of death and wound the reins about the brake handle. 'We'll wait here,' he said. They would be burying the bodies now. What was it Donaldson had said? *For the seven hundred miles of the trail there are one and a half graves per mile.*

The wind moaned through the telegraph wires. Behind them some of the troopers had appeared, riding slowly toward the trail. The white tilts of the wagons showed up over the ridge.

'You plan to go to Oregon alone?' Sabin asked.

'Yes.'

'It's a long way.'

'It's a long way back. Not in miles but in thoughts.'

'I see,' he said. 'What will you do out there?'

83

'Teach school if I can. I'll find work.'

'What about Colonel Bascomb?'

Her hands closed tightly. 'If I were a man I'd seek him out,' she said.

'Let him alone. He's not to be trifled with.'

'You know him then?'

'Yes. I know him.'

She leaned back against a wagon bow. 'His daughter paid me to help her,' she said. 'She's beautiful.'

He nodded. 'I know.'

She turned her head to scrutinize him more directly. 'You're a strange man, Sabin Shay.'

He smiled. 'Why do you say that?'

'You're not a Yankee.'

'No.'

'Jonas Scribner said you were a Galvanized Yankee.'

'Do you dislike me for that?'

'All I know is that you've been kind to a woman who is alone in the world.'

'*Gracias*,' he said dryly. 'I was brought up right, I suppose.'

'Yes. Beneath that hard face there seems to be a gentleness, Sabin Shay.'

He shrugged and got down from the seat. He looked up at her. 'Take my advice. Find a man and get married if you insist on going through to Oregon.'

'I need no man!'

'So? You'll see. You'll be all right to Fort Laramie. You must make your own way from then on.'

'You'll stay there?'

'Who knows? The Yanks may want us to—'

Cobb Howell cantered up and drew rein. He doffed his cap. 'Afternoon, Miss Katherine.'

'Good afternoon, Cobb Howell.'

Cobb eyed her in appreciation. 'The major wants we should scout ahead, Sabin.'

He untied his horse and mounted, kneeing it close to the girl. 'It's dangerous out here, Miss Katherine. Keep your guns handy. I know you know how to use them.'

'It's more dangerous where you're going.'

He smiled. 'Most of my life has been that way, Miss Katherine. But I'd like you to have a future.' He tipped his cap and followed the big Texan along the telegraph line. After a while he looked back. She waved to him.

CHAPTER TEN

It had been over seven years since Sabin had seen old Fort Laramie. He had equipped himself there in '58 for the gold rush to Cherry Creek, two hundred miles south of the post. He had still been weak from the fever which had struck him down in the early fall of '57 while hunting in the Cheyenne country.

Donaldson's dusty column lined up on the parade ground while Donaldson went to arrange quarters for them. Sabin stepped out of ranks and took inventory. Old Bedlam, the two-story stone officers' quarters had received a fresh coat of whitewash. The fort squatted on a huge paw-shaped bluff with the pewter colored waters of the Laramie washing its base. New barracks had been added, and at the foot of the bluff, to the northeast, he noticed many additional buildings: quartermaster store-houses, a post office, commissary warehouse, a mill yard, laundry, sadler's workshop, quartermaster quarters, a blacksmith shop, teamster's quarters and a corral with blockhouses at opposite corners. Lines of Sibley tents bellied in the fresh breeze.

The original walled fort, Old Fort John, was now used as the commanding officer's quarters. Behind the quartermaster storehouse, Sabin saw lines of emigrant wagons. He walked past the barracks and looked down on them. Sway-backed Conestogas, smaller models of the same efficient type, Studebakers, and a miscellaneous group of bastard types. At one end of a line of nine splendid modified Conestogas he spied an anachronism—a covered Dearborn, shining in the sun. His heart caught. Colonel Bascomb had nine wagons and a Dearborn in his private train.

She was here!

'Shay!' bellowed Sergeant Schmidt. 'You think maybe you don'dt haff to stay in ranks yedt?'

Sabin grinned as he strolled back to the ranks. Schmidt had big fists planted on his hips. 'You men listen here! You haff been on the trail many days! Diss place is to gedt rest and fix op equipmendt yedt! There iss vimmens here! Vhite vimmens and redt vimmens! Dere ain'dt no way I can vatch you twenty-four hours a day! You vill fool mit dese vimmens and gedt into trouble yedt! This I cannot shtop! But vhen Virst Call comes, you vill be in the ranks, ready to do a day'ss vork, or I vill show you who iss the boss here! There are plenty of vagon wheels to lash you to! There iss plenty of sandt to fill your haversacks so you shouldt carry it roundt and roundt the parade groundt! Drunk, sober, or just plain lazy, you vill act like soldiers yedt, or Manfred Schmidt ain'dt topkick of diss J Company oudfidt! Remember diss!'

'Damn Dutchman,' Cob Howell said out of the side of his mouth.

'He knows his business,' Sabin said. 'I'll give him credit for that much.'

Donaldson came back to his command. Orders rippled out. The infantrymen slogged off to an empty barracks. The wagons rolled down to the area near the Q.M. warehouse.

87

The cavalry led their horses to the corrals and then carried their mass of gear to a line of faded, sagging Sibleys.

Sabin dumped his gear on a rickety cot and inspected his new quarters. The canvas was riddled with scorched holes from careless firemaking. Cobb Howell stooped to get into the tent. 'Damn!' he said. 'I thought these Yanks had good equipment. This tent would make a good fish net.'

'Thank the Lord for small favors,' intoned cadaverous Blalock Lott. 'I'll match you for the cot nearest the door, Brother Howell.'

'Stable frocks!' yelled a non-com out in the company street. 'Let's get at them horses, Johnnies! You ain't in no Rebel critter company. You're in the U.S. Cavalry, by Gawd!'

'*Cavalry*,' Howell sneered. 'The dumb booger can't even pronounce it right. Should be *calvary*!'

Warner Giddings stumbled into the tent laden with his gear. 'Damn Yankees take soldiering serious,' he said. 'Yuh see them Pawnees down behint the officers' stables? Must be a hunnert of 'em. Pawnee Scouts.'

Cobb Howell twirled the cylinder of his Colt. 'One of these days,' he said, 'I'll help that little Williams gal to even up the score.'

Sabin glanced toward the Dearborn as he trudged to the stables carrying his horse-cleaning gear. A woman was riding sidesaddle toward the line of wagons. She wore a modish riding costume of Army blue. A forage cap was tilted to one side of her honey-colored hair. The sun glinted on the crossed saber insignia on the cap. Sabin stopped and stared hungrily at Marianne Bascomb. There had been a time when Marianne had promised a kiss to every Confederate who would bring her news of killing a bluebelly. Times had certainly changed in the family of Colonel Bascomb.

★   ★   ★

The horses had been cleaned and fed. The Sibleys had been swept out. The bunks had been made and the equipment had been cleaned and put away. Sabin had bathed in the cold river and had hacked away his beard. He hooked the collar of his jacket and placed his forage cap on his head.

Blalock Lott sat on his bunk in his baggy gray drawers, industriously cleaning his carbine barrel. He eyed Sabin and then winked at Cobb Howell. 'The bird of paradise goes forth,' he said.

Howell lay on his bunk with his hands behind his head. 'Keep away from them squaws,' he said with a grin, 'or they'll leave yuh with a memento of Fort Laramie yuh ain't about to like.'

Warner Giddings blew gently into his

trumpet. 'Hell,' he said. 'He ain't foolin' with no breed doxie. I seen him eyeing that filly riding about here with the forage cap on her *cabeza*. Cap'n Shay likes class.'

'Shut up,' Sabin said sourly. 'You bastards talk too much.'

He left the tent and struck off toward the parade ground. A quartermaster corporal had told him the Bascombs had taken up quarters in an unused officer's quarters. Trust old Colonel Bascomb to deal himself in on the best.

The sun was long gone. Lights had sprung up all over the sprawling post. The wind was cold as it swept across the bluff. Sabin looked down at his uniform. He wondered what Marianne Bascomb would think of Private Sabin Shay, United States Cavalry. She always did have a penchant for epaulets, sashes and swords.

A slim man leaned against a post in front of Bascomb's quarters, puffing at a cigar. He wore a wide-awake hat on the back of his fine blond hair. A neat broadcloth suit with the trousers tucked into polished Hersome gaiters. A splash of white linen showed at his throat.

Sabin stopped. 'Good evening, Stacy,' he said quietly.

Stacy Bascomb straightened up. 'This is Officer's Row, soldier,' he said coldly. 'Are you here on duty?'

Then the Louisianian bent his head forward and stared at Sabin. 'You called me by name. By God! It's Sabin Shay!'

Sabin nodded. 'I just came in with Donaldson.'

Bewilderment showed on the handsome spoiled face of Stacy Bascomb. 'You? In a Yankee uniform? What is this?'

'They call us Galvanized Yankees, Stacy.'

Bascomb threw away his cigar. 'Damned traitors!' he snapped.

Sabin went cold. 'What are *you* doing here on a U.S. post? Where's your militia uniform, Stacy? The nice clean one that never got stained by sweat, mud and blood?'

Bascomb jerked his fine head. 'I was paroled,' he said, 'according to the rules of war.'

'You know a helluva lot about war, militiaman.'

Thin lines were etched on Stacy's face. He slid his right hand inside his coat.

Sabin grinned. 'You haven't got the guts to draw on me, sonny. I'll take that hideout gun away from you and break your head with it. Where's Marianne?'

'Inside. You'd better keep away from her, suh. Father won't like it.'

'I'm worried.'

Stacy Bascomb withdrew his hand. Then he smiled thinly. He bowed. 'Mister Shay,' he said politely, 'do present yourself.

Marianne may have something to say to you.'

Sabin walked past the immaculate Louisianian. He tapped on the door while Stacy lit a fresh cigar. The flare of the lucifer illuminated the sly grin on his face.

A gaunt woman opened the door. 'Yes?'

'I'd like to see Miss Bascomb.'

'Who's a-callin'?'

'Tell her it's a good friend.'

The woman shrugged and plodded on flat feet into a rear hallway. Sabin looked about. A fire crackled on the hearth. Soft rugs covered most of the rough wooden floor. The place was of field officer grade.

A door opened and Marianne Bascomb came into the room. Breath caught in Sabin's throat. She had gained beauty in the years since he had last seen her. Her figure had filled out. She wore a low-cut silk dress which exposed the deep cleavage between her full breasts.

'Sabin Shay!' she said. 'What are you doing heah in *that* uniform?'

He held out a hand, wanting to touch her. She made no effort to approach him. She looked from side to side in confusion. 'This is a shock,' she said.

'I've come from Fort MacNaughton, Marianne. I'd hoped you'd be here.'

She placed a hand at her throat. 'I don't understand.'

'It's simple. I took the oath of allegiance

and enlisted for frontier service.'

'But you had your own company, Sabin! You were a Confederate officer!'

He grinned ruefully. 'Now you don't think the United States would give me bars after my fighting them for nearly four years!'

Lord, but she was beautiful. The hard days on the trail had done nothing to harm her freshness. Sabin stood there, almost like a schoolboy, turning his forage cap round and round in his big hands, devouring her with his eyes.

She flushed. She knew what was in his mind. She had held nothing back from him in the old courting days. Now he was here like a lean, wind-burned ghost, wearing an alien uniform, expecting her to feel as she had in New Orleans.

She looked past him. 'Father is due back here any moment,' she said. 'We're to dine with Colonel Collins.'

'I saw you this afternoon,' he said desperately.

She walked to a window. 'You can't bring back the past, Sabin.'

'Why? We were in love. We were to be married when the war was over.'

She turned her head a little. Her fine white teeth pressed into her lower lip. 'So many things have changed,' she said uncertainly.

A wave of utter loneliness swept over him. He walked close to her, fearing to touch her, not knowing how far he would go.

She raised her head. 'Father plans a new life in Oregon,' she said quickly.

'I may be planning that very thing myself, Marianne.'

He placed his hands on her smooth white shoulders. For a moment it seemed as though she might come to him and then she moved away from him.

'What's wrong, Marianne?'

She spoke over her shoulder. 'Father and Stacy don't want me to associate with old friends.'

'I see,' he said quietly.

She whirled around. 'It isn't what you think! The Confederacy is doomed! There was nothing to be gained by staying in New Orleans. Father might have been ruined. He was clever enough to get his family out of there and get permission to come west. He can't afford to take chances now, Sabin.'

It hit him like a dose of canister. Then he came back fighting. He stepped close to her, slid his left arm about her waist and pulled her close. Her head went back and her full lips met his in a long bruising kiss that had the old-time fire in it. Then she pushed at him frantically. 'Things have changed, Sabin. They've changed, I tell you!'

He turned her face toward his and kissed her again. Then he pressed his cheek to hers, feeling the wetness of tears. 'We can start again,' he said softly. 'Out in Oregon.'

She broke away from him. 'Father mustn't see you here.'

He smiled. 'Dear Stacy has already seen me.'

She waved a hand toward the door. 'Please go. I'll tell Father that you came by to see me and I sent you away.'

'But you *haven't*, Marianne.'

Her lips parted. 'No. I'll get word to you when I can see you.'

He closed the door behind him. A man walked toward the quarters. Sabin walked across the porch. Stacy Bascomb grinned in the shadows. 'Heah comes Father, Shay,' he said with relish. 'It's a damned good thing for you, suh, that he didn't come in on you and my sister.'

Colonel Bascomb stopped short when he saw Sabin. 'Sabin Shay! Befo' God, suh! What are you doing heah?'

Sabin bowed. 'I might ask you the same thing, sir.'

Bascomb slowly took the cigar from his plump lips. 'A damned Galvanized Yankee!' he said.

'A Reconstructed Rebel,' Sabin said in return.

'Suh?'

Stacy moved out of the shadows. 'He means you Father.'

Colonel Bascomb looked quickly about to

see if anyone was within earshot. 'You will watch that kind of talk, suh!' he said furiously. 'Furthermore, my daughter is not for your sort.'

Sabin slanted his forage cap on his head. '*My* sort? What must she think of a man who would deliberately desert a sick man out on the trail—a man who died because of your callousness?'

Bascomb dropped his cigar. His mustaches and goatee seemed to bristle. 'You mean Williams, suh? The man was hopelessly ill with Asiatic cholera. There was no hope for him. None at all, suh. I did not want to endanger my family.'

Sabin shook his head. 'He had pneumonia. The Pawnees came down on them near Chimney Rock. They killed the boy and tied the father to a wagon wheel. Then they set the wagon afire. He burned alive, Bascomb! Katherine Williams was saved from a hellish fate because we came up just in time. *You* talk about *my* sort? Look into your own soul, Bascomb. God help you when you realize what you've done!'

Stacy came forward and faced Sabin. 'I'd ask you out, suh,' he said stiffly, 'if you were a gentleman!'

Sabin's right hand cracked across the handsome face in front of him. 'You haven't got the guts of a cottontail,' he said. 'Get out of my way.'

Bascomb raised his left hand to his stinging face. Shock filmed his blue eyes. His father shifted a little.

Sabin shouldered Stacy aside. 'Colonel,' he said quietly, 'keep your hands out of your pockets.'

Clay Bascomb slowly took out a silver cigar case. 'Get out of heah,' he said softly. 'An enlisted man has no business heah unless he's on duty. I'll have you thrown into the guardhouse, suh!'

'No need. I'm going.' Sabin turned on a heel. He walked across the parade ground, then down the slope toward the tent lines. He skirted the end of the wagon line where slab-sided men and gaunt women moved about. He looked toward Katherine's wagon. She wasn't in sight.

A big infantryman from the Kansas Volunteers leaned against a wagon. 'There's one of 'em now,' he said to some emigrant men lounging near him. 'One of them Texicans who joined up.'

Sabin walked past. The Kansan grinned. 'He was an officer from what I hear tell,' he said loudly. 'Another damn Rebel crawlin' back into blue before the war ends. State's Rights! Hawwww!'

Sabin stopped.

The Kansan was big and cocky. He thrust out his chest. 'Well?' he challenged.

One of the civilians grinned. 'He looks

97

right purty in blue,' he said.

'Shore does,' said another with a wink.

Sabin eyed them. 'I don't see you two clay-eaters in uniform,' he said. 'Are you bounty jumpers or just plain yellow?'

The soldier waved a restraining hand at the two red-faced civilians. He swaggered close to Sabin. 'I'm your oyster,' he said. 'Leave the boys alone, Galvanized Yankee. I hate the guts of any man as turns against his country, even if it is that stinkin' Confederacy.'

All the accumulated hatred for the Bascombs welled up in Sabin like a deep maroon flood. He smashed a left into the Kansan's gut and followed through with a right uppercut which snapped back his opponent's head. The soldier crashed back against the wagon and went down. He shook his head. One of the civilians snatched up a broken wagon tongue and swung it at Sabin. The jagged tip slashed Sabin's face. He went under the tongue and smashed two blows home to the gut. The man grunted and dropped the wagon tongue. He went down on one knee and Sabin finished his interest in the fight by planting a heel against his slack jaw.

Sabin whirled to meet a wavering attack from the first civilian. It was easy. Hate powered the swift blows. The man went down with a smashed nose. 'I had enough,' he yelled.

Sabin stepped back and looked at the

crowd. 'Anyone else?' he asked thickly.

A gaunt bearded man came forward. 'I'm Sam Nelson. Wagonmaster. Go back to your quarters, soldier. We got nothin' against yuh. Clem Barton and Bill Ryland are troublemakers.'

'Thanks.' Sabin looked down at the bloody human wreckage he had created. Somehow he felt better.

Katherine Williams stood beside her wagon as he walked away. 'Let me bathe that face, Sabin Shay,' she said.

'I'm all right.'

'Please,' she said.

'Forget it. You're amongst your own people now. They don't like Galvanized Yankees.'

'I speak for myself, Sabin.'

He walked away into the shadows.

CHAPTER ELEVEN

Trouble came to roost on the roof tops of lonely Fort Laramie, flapping its ragged wings in sensuous pleasure, scanning the curious mixture of humans which inhabited the post. There were hard-shelled Abolitionists and Kansas Free-Soilers; Union Volunteers from Kansas, Ohio, Iowa, Michigan and Missouri; tobacco-spitting

99

emigrants from a dozen different states; veteran regulars and green militia. Now a new ingredient had been added to the mixture. Lean-jawed, hard-pratted men of a different breed, somehow alien in dusty blue. Men who looked as though they had been living in a smoky suburb of hell for too long a time.

Trouble had seen the likes of these men before. Fighting at the Alamo, Goliad and San Jacinto. Tangling with whooping Comanches and Lipans. Leading the wild assaults of Lee's infantry as members of the famed First, Fourth and Fifth Texas of Hood's Division, coupled with the Third Arkansas, rated as some of the best shock troops in the Confederate Army.

These new inhabitants of Fort Laramie were no Johnny Raws, who had yet to pop their first caps in battle. There weren't many of them, but it had been said that they would charge hell with a bucket of water. Trouble looked at the lowering sky. Rain always played hell at these Western outposts. Good! The rain would set the mood just fine.

The rain started gently, pattering on the shake roofs and stippling the shallow waters of the Laramie. It marbled the windows of the post buildings and changed the color of the faded canvas tents. It slicked the talmas of the men on guard. By noon it had begun to soak the post thoroughly. Then it shifted into a heavier downpour as the Thunder People

100

loosed their eerie shafts of lightning across the streaming hills. The gutters ran and pools formed in the low spots on the wide parade ground. Now it was a real, rousing rain.

Pay call had blown at Fort Laramie that afternoon. The eagle had flown over and deposited two months pay. Trouble patiently added this to the brew. It couldn't be more perfect. Rain and payday. There was one more vital ingredient. Whiskey. There was plenty of it at the sutler's. The soldiers had money and no duties to perform. The brew was ready for the tasting.

Cobb Howell splashed through the mud of the company street and entered the sagging Sibley. He shot a hard glance at the perforated canvas. Blalock Lott perched on his bunk, huddled under his talma, gloomily smoking his pipe. Warner Giddings was counting his pay. Sabin Shay was covering his bunk with one of the Yankee shelter halves. Cobb spat out into the streaming street.

'I'm buyin',' he said, 'I'm sick of lookin' at your constipated faces.'

Lott looked up. 'The demon Rum has no appeal to me, as a rule, Brother Howell, but it seems to me that a little spirits might help me. Take a little wine for thy stomach's sake, and thine infirmities.'

Giddings slid his pay into his pocket. 'I'm game,' he said.

'I'll pass,' Sabin said.

The three Texans splashed up the company street. Here and there another Texan came out of a tent and followed them. Sabin hooked his talma and slanted his forage cap over his right eye. There was no damned use staying in the tent. The wind bellied the soaked canvas and flapped the fly.

Sabin waded through the mud toward the emigrant wagons. He hadn't seen Katherine Williams since the evening of his fight with the Kansan and his civilian allies. He had been damned short with her. He scratched on the canvas of her wagon.

A slab-sided emigrant woman poked her head out of her dripping wagon. 'She ain't there, soljer,' she said. 'Went up to the fort. That Bascomb woman sent for her.'

Sabin walked up the greasy path and came out at the eastern end of Officers' Row. The rain slanted down finely. The low sutler's building was ablaze with lights. For a moment Sabin was almost tempted to get a drink or two, but he didn't want Katherine to listen to his apologies and smell the liquor on his breath at the same time. He slogged toward Bascomb's quarters. He'd wait until she was free. Liquor had been flowing like the rain all day and both soldiers and civilians were carrying plenty of the potent stuff. There weren't enough women to go around at Laramie; particularly a good-looking woman like Katherine Williams.

Old Bedlam, the bachelor officers' quarters, was well lit up, and the music of a gay polka came from the dance orchestra. Sabin stopped beside one of the streaming windows. He looked in at the small dance floor, packed to the nines with dancing couples. He saw Marianne Bascomb, with flushed and laughing face whirl by in the arms of a captain, and then a shock hit him as he recognized the face of Frank Khuyper bending over that of Marianne.

He turned away into the rain and darkness. It all figured. A woman like Marianne would be fair quarry for every bachelor officer on the post. Frank Khuyper was handsome enough to catch any woman's eye.

Suddenly Sabin wondered about Katherine Williams. The emigrant woman had said Marianne had sent for Katherine. Yet the dance had been on for quite some time. She should have been back with her own people by now. Sabin walked swiftly toward the Bascomb's quarters, feeling uneasy.

The living room of the Bascombs was dimly lit. Sabin stepped up on the porch, raised his hand to knock, then lowered it. He didn't want a scene with the old man or Stacy. Khuyper still had the power to give him a bitch of a time, and one word or two from Clay Bascomb would start the persecution.

Sabin peered through a rain dappled

window. There was a low settee in front of the blazing fire. A shapely head showed above the back. A man stood at the end of the fireplace with his arm resting on the mantel, talking to the woman. For the second time within a matter of minutes Sabin felt a ball of ice in his gut. The woman was Katherine and the man was Stacy.

It hit him hard. He wanted to smash in the door and grip Stacy by his smooth throat and squeeze his rotten life out of him. He wanted to take Katherine Williams. His big hands opened and closed at his sides. Then reason regained the saddle, slipped the bit in his mouth, and led him away.

He walked down Officers' Row to the magazine at the far end, and stepped into the shelter of the overhanging roof to wait for Katherine. Minutes ticked past. Now and then he stepped out into the drizzle for a better view but there was nothing but the rain, the beating of the orchestra in the dance hall, and the din from the sutler's store.

Half an hour passed. Then he saw her walking toward him. He stepped out into the rain just as a man burst out of the sutler's and plashed past. 'Oh, man!' he said as he raced past, 'There's hell to pay in the sutler's. Some of them Galvanized Yankees tangled with some of the Kansas and Missouri boys. Old Silk the bartender is out cold!'

The guard broke from the provost-marshal's building and double-timed through the rain toward the sutlery. Sabin lost sight of Katherine. He walked toward the sutlery. The guard was wasting no time. They were used to pay nights at Fort Laramie. Carbine butts thudded home, laying a bloody carpet of drunken battlers on the dirty floor.

The sergeant of the guard surveyed the havoc. 'Dammit, Silk,' he said to the weaving bartender. 'We ain't got room for *all* of 'em in the guardhouse.'

Silk spat bloodily. 'Just clear 'em outa here, Donovan. That's all I ask. I'm closin'!'

The guards were grinning as they hauled the subdued battlers to their feet and shoved them through the doorway into the soaked street. Sabin saw Blalock Lott. His face was battered and bloody. Big Cobb Howell rubbed abraded knuckles against his hips and winked at Sabin. He stooped and slung little Warner Giddings over his shoulder. The kid was out cold.

The shambling drunks weaved past Old Bedlam. The porch was crowded with the finely dressed ladies and immaculate officers of the post, eyeing the doleful procession. Sabin walked behind the guard. He saw Marianne Bascomb.

Frank Khuyper came to the edge of the porch. 'What happened, sergeant?' he asked harshly.

Donovan saluted. 'Payday is all, sir.'

'Lock them up. Every mother's son of them.' Khuyper's hard eyes spotted Sabin. 'That tall one! Why isn't he under guard?'

Donovan turned quickly. '*Him*, sir? He wasn't mixed up in the fracas.'

Khuyper bit his lip. 'Place the rest of them in the cells. Bread and water. Buck and gag them!'

Donovan looked curiously at Khuyper. 'I'm sorry, sir. But the colonel has standing orders for these payday Donnybrooks. Unless someone is badly hurt we usually send the boys back to their organizations.'

Khuyper fumed. 'Discipline seems to be damned loose around here.'

Donovan couldn't help but speak up. 'The men involved in the fight came in with Major Donaldson's command,' he said.

Khuyper went white. Marianne Bascomb slid a smooth arm under his,. 'Frank,' she said, 'we have the next polka.'

Sabin grinned. Khuyper saw the grin. For a moment it seemed as though he would tear himself away from her to vent his cruelty on some of the poor sots standing in the pouring rain. Then he followed her inside.

Donovan spat. 'Now you misbegotten sons of hardcase bitches! You thick-headed sons of Belial! You cotton-mouthed slobs! Get back to your quarters and thank God for an understanding commanding officer!'

'Scratch my hairy rump,' said Warner

Giddings from Howell's shoulder.

Donovan nodded at a big private of the guard. 'Take that one,' he said, and eyed the rest of the Galvanized Yankees. 'Anyone else?'

There was no answer. The guard carried Giddings toward the guardhouse.

Donovan inflated his barrel chest. 'I'm a Regular,' he said. 'I don't like volunteers and militia. But I'm a Yankee. I hear of anymore trouble outa you Galvanized Yankees and I'll run the whole damn lot of you in.'

'Go to hell, Donovan!' Giddings called back.

The battered Texans stood in the rain watching Giddings being taken to the pokey. 'Never could keep his mouth shut, that boy,' Howell said.

Sabin walked with them down the greasy path. He stopped at the foot of it. 'I'll see you later,' he said, and went toward the dripping wagons.

He hunched deeper in his talma as the rain sluiced down. His head snapped up as he heard a woman scream from an outbuilding near the wagon line. Two men were fighting savagely in the darkness. One of them thudded a club down on the head of the other then raised the club for a killing blow as his opponent went down into thick mud. Sabin closed in behind him, reached over his shoulder and snatched away the club. The

107

man whirled. Sabin saw the dim contorted face of Matt Duggan. A sour stench of whiskey flooded over him. He chopped hard with the club. Duggan fell down over his victim.

Sabin stepped back. Katherine Williams stood in the doorway of the outbuilding, holding her ripped dress together with shaking hands. 'He followed me from the Bascombs,' she said.

Sabin knelt by the side of the man Duggan had felled. It was Sergeant Manfred Schmidt. His swollen face was blood-streaked. He opened his eyes. 'It wass you who savedt me, Shay?'

Sabin nodded.

'Thanks. Gedt the guardt. This man shouldt be in the guardthouse.'

Sabin trotted up the path to the guardhouse. Donovan was at the door having a smoke. 'Sergeant Schmidt was attacked by Trooper Matthew Duggan,' Sabin said. 'I dropped Duggan. Get down there and get him in the wagon yard before he comes to, or it will take most of your guard to subdue him.'

Schmidt was leaning against the outbuilding when Sabin returned. 'I prefer charges,' he said thickly. 'That man iss not righdt in the headt. You agree?'

'Yes.'

Schmidt picked up his mud-plastered cap.

'He might haff killdt me. I don'dt forget, Shay.'

Sabin watched Schmidt walk off into the darkness. He turned angrily to Katherine. 'I once told you to find a man and get married if you intended to go on to Oregon,' he said harshly.

She fumbled with the front of her dress and then pulled her cape over the wreckage. 'I need no man,' she said.

'I said you'd be all right until we reached Fort Laramie. This sort of thing can happen any time. There are many men here without women. There are women who will play along with them. Most of these men don't know the difference between a good woman and a bad one.'

'Do you?'

He stared at her. 'Yes. I think I do.'

She walked toward her wagon. 'Are you still in love with Marianne Bascomb, Sabin Shay?'

He felt as if he had been slapped hard across the face. 'You know about us then?'

'Yes.'

'Who told you?'

She stopped at her wagon. 'Stacy.'

'He would.'

She looked curiously at him. 'I suspected as much. I've been helping her with her hair and wardrobe. Once I mentioned your name and she said she'd known you very well in New

Orleans.'

Sabin leaned against the wagon. 'You seem to be on friendly enough terms with the Bascombs after what they allowed to happen to your father.'

'Stacy explained to me that his father had an inordinate horror of Asiatic cholera. Stacy's mother died of it when he was a boy, and Colonel Bascomb worshipped her. He lost his head and left us. I've tried to forgive him, Sabin.'

'My God,' Sabin said involuntarily. He controlled himself. 'I'm sorry, Katherine.'

She touched his face with a cool wet hand. 'You always seem to be around when I need you.'

She put her hands on his shoulders, drew him down and planted a soft kiss on his mouth. Then his loneliness swept over him again. He drew her close and kissed her hard. She tried to push him back but he kissed her again and again, stopping only when her hand cracked wetly against his face. 'Let me alone,' she said. 'You're like all the rest.'

Sabin walked away with the fires still flaring in his mind. He looked back at her. She was so damned alone, and fair game for a smooth talker like Stacy Bascomb. Sabin wondered if he should tell Katherine the real story of Therese Bascomb. He knew the facts, all right. Colonel Bascomb had been just as much responsible for *her* death as he had been for Katherine's father and brother.

Lott was asleep in the leaking tent. Howell was hunched in his talma with a bottle between his wet knees. Sabin took it and drank deeply. 'To hell with everything,' he said.

Lott opened one discolored eye. 'Amen,' he said.

The rain beat down steadily. Trouble had had a good day. He shook the water from his ragged wings and flitted silently north through the sluicing rain. Up there in the north, Sioux, Cheyennes and Arapahoes were hunching in their wet lodges, bitterly re-telling the tales of the white man's perfidy. The odds were with him.

CHAPTER TWELVE

At any ordinary Army post, in any ordinary military district, Matt Duggan would have been tried properly by general court-martial. But this was Fort Laramie on the Oregon Trail. Somehow the formal court-martial became a drumhead affair—and somehow Captain Frank Khuyper became a member of the court, while the presiding officer turned out to be the sort of over-age-in-grade, whiskey-sodden political time-server who could be 'spared' from more rigorous tactical

111

duties.

The court could do nothing less than sustain the charges of attempted rape and assault upon a non-commissioned officer with a deadly weapon. The facts and the witnesses were on hand, and the verdict had to be Guilty As Charged. But after the witnesses departed, after the officers of the court were free to talk at leisure over a comradely drink, prior to passing sentence, something went wrong.

Next day, Matt Duggan's head was shaved. Then he was drummed out of the service to the tune of the Rogue's March. He had been given a dishonorable discharge with ritual trimmings, and that was all. Duggan took up his residence among other scum who lived with 'Ration Indians'—lazy fullbloods and diseased half-breeds—beside the Laramie, downslope from the officers' stables. The Galvanized Yankees came to a high Texas boil inside their bluebelly uniforms. They talked of killing Matt Duggan.

Sabin Shay took it hardest of all, but he had to stay calm.

'Listen,' he said. 'I know it's a mockery of justice and I know Khuyper's behind it. But hear this. Khuyper did it in the hope that we'd bust loose in garrison. He'd like nothing better than to se us kill Duggan. Then he could have us hanged for it.'

Warner Giddings knitted his brows in

112

strenuous thought.

'Well,' he said, 'leastways it shows how a fellow can get out of this dirtyshirt blue. Now suppose I was just to up an' gunwhip some bluebelly non-com—'

'No!' Sabin said. 'In Duggan's case, Khuyper had it easy. He could remind those fools that Federal prisons in the East are already bulging with Rebels. He could predict that they'll all be turned loose automatically, once the war's over, the criminal as well as the non-criminal. He could point out that transport back over the trail is in such a fix that taking the cost and trouble to ship a guarded prisoner back East would be virtually a crime in itself. He could argue that a Rebel who'd taken the Federal oath would be a pariah in Texas right now, and that with a dishonorable discharge from the Federal Army thrown in, he wouldn't even dare to go home. You see?'

'I guess so,' Giddings said. 'He tricked them into thinkin' the easy way out was just to turn Duggan loose here, stranded-like. But why wouldn't it work—'

'For the rest of us? Because a second crime would expose their mistake and they'd have to get tough. Slug a non-com, Warner, and they'll put you behind bars for a long, long time. Kill Matt Duggan and you'll hang. Khuyper knows it. Now don't play into his hands—any of you. We've got to wait.

Understand?'

They understood. They left Duggan alone. And they waited.

The roads were still too muddy for travel. The emigrants still camped at the post, having babies, squabbling amongst themselves, raising hell in general. A few cavalry patrols splashed off on the muddy roads. The telegraph line went out regularly as the Indians cut it. Katherine Williams worked for Marianne Bascomb, and Marianne Bascomb worked on Captain Frank Khuyper, and Matt Duggan got himself a job as teamster with Colonel Bascomb.

Robert E. Lee attacked Fort Stedman on the Union right at Petersburg, according to a telegraph dispatch from the East, and failed. General 'Jube' Early ran afoul of Phil Sheridan at Waynesboro and lost most of his command. Sheridan cut the Virginia Central and the James River Canal. 'Cump' Sherman was chasing Joe Johnston as the strong Federal force under his command moved toward Fayetteville for the eventual junction with U. S. Grant.

Sabin Shay went about his duties with a sickness in his soul. The South had no hope left now. He knew it and the men knew it. All they could do was go on waiting, biding their time for the chance to leave this fort behind and strike out West for themselves.

At night, Sabin always walked across the

parade ground to the edge of the Laramie bluffs and spent a while alone, staring blindly west into the windy darkness. A man cannot follow a flag for four years and then suddenly admit that the flag no longer exists. Soon the smoke-blackened, shot-torn Stars and Bars would be a trophy in the Yankees' hands. But he had to get used to the idea, to cure his soul sickness, to search out a new aim in life that meant more than just a purposeless flight into the Western nowhere.

He was trying, but it would take time.

CHAPTER THIRTEEN

Sabin picked up the heavy ration box and hoisted it to his bruised shoulder. He settled it and trudged out of the stifling warehouse into the quartermaster wagon yard. Cobb Howell poked his head out from the rear of the wagon. 'How many more of them damned boxes?' he asked.

Sabin plumped the box down on the tailgate.

'Watch that box!' roared a corporal. 'You'll be eating some of those rations out on the trail starting tomorrow!'

Cobb wiped the sweat from his face and spat at a lantern hanging on the warehouse wall. 'Yuh know what *yuh* kin do, yuh

Yankee snotnose,' he said in a low voice.

'That's the last,' Sabin said. He wiped his dirty forehead with the back of his left forearm. 'What time is it?'

Cobb dropped from the tailgate into the churned mud of the yard. 'I heard Call To Quarters awhile back. Ain't time for yuh to make the dance, Sabin.'

Sabin looked down at his filthy stable frock. He itched. He needed a shave. 'I told Katherine Williams I'd pick her up at eight for the enlisted men's dance.'

Cobb shifted his chew of spit-or-drown. 'Yeh. There's a skunk in the woodpile, Sabin. That slick Bascomb kid prob'ly whispered a few choice words into Khuyper's dirty ear. Worked fine too. Here yuh are standing in manure and mud, smelling near as bad as the manure, when you're supposed to be squirin' Miss Williams to the dance.'

The two-striper sloshed through the mud. 'That all?' he snapped.

'We ain't standin' here whilst there's work to be done!' Cobb said to mock horror. 'Now you know thet, *sir!*'

The corporal bent his brows. Cobb had been riding him all evening, and he wasn't quite sure what to do about it. 'All right,' he said. 'Haul your butts outa here. See you get cleaned up, too. We head west at dawn.'

Cobb thrust out a thick arm. 'Forward to glory!' he crowed.

Sabin couldn't help but grin as he trudged through the mud with the big Texan. It was hard to beat Cobb Howell down. If he liked you it was easy to handle him; if he didn't like you, he could give you hell's own time.

'There ain't been nothin' but trouble for you since Stacy Bascomb's been butterin' up Miss Williams,' Cobb said.

'There was plenty of it before we ever got to Fort Laramie, Cobb.'

Cobb shot a sideways glance at him. 'Yeh. But you been gettin' it from all angles. It's a queer world, Cap'n Shay.'

They entered the company street. Cobb placed a hand on Sabin's shoulder. 'One of these days yore luck will change.'

'What the hell are you driving at?'

Cobb stopped and faced Sabin. 'Bad enough Khuyper had it in fer yuh at MacNaughton. Now he's squirin' Miss Bascomb around. That filly is enough to unhinge a man's mind, ef'n she has a mind to, and it shore looks like she has.'

Sabin flushed. 'Take care,' he warned in a low voice.

Cobb shook his head. 'We're amigos, Cap'n Shay. I want thet yuh should know that all the time. But yuh got a bot fly borin' into yuh with this Bascomb woman. It ain't right. What with her switchin' that rump of hers all over the post and hangin' on to Khuyper's arm like he was God hisself.'

Sabin swung from the hip, but Howell had been expecting it. He blocked the hard blow with a thick forearm and wrapped a bear hug about Sabin. Then he spoke with his face a few inches away from Sabin's. 'Damn yuh! The boys been wrathy about yuh. They know what's been eatin' yuh. Can't yuh see what's goin' on? Now *listen* for a change, instead of talkin'!' Cobb stepped back and placed his hand on his hips.

Sabin controlled himself.

Howell looked up and down the quiet street. Most of the men had gone to the dance thrown for those leaving the post for duty on the trail. 'Yuh ain't nothin' but a draggle-assed high private in the rear rank of a John company, Sabin. Not *Captain* Shay, of Shay's Independent Frontier Company! That Bascomb gal is wise. Her old man got her outa New Orleans whilst the gettin' was good. Headin' for Oregon and a new life. Now is she goin' to take up with a Galvanized Yankee out there? Hell no! Not whilst she can hitch herself to *Captain* Frank Khuyper. By God, Sabin, she may still like yuh. *Love* yuh, for all I know. But there ain't no place in her nest fer yuh. Get *thet* through yore hard *cabeza*!'

'Go to hell,' Sabin said sourly, and walked toward his tent.

He cleaned himself swiftly and scraped off his beard. He dressed and left the tent. He found Howell sitting on a box at the end of

118

the street, sucking at his battered pipe. Howell grinned at Sabin. 'A fine night,' he ventured.

Sabin stopped. 'Somewhere along the line,' he said, 'You seem to have forgotten that I asked Katherine Williams to the dance tonight.'

'Appears like I did. Howsomever, Cap'n Shay, I been with yuh quite a spell now. I saw yuh read that jasmine smellin' letter damned near every night whilst we was on the trail to here from Fort MacNaughton. I've seen yuh look at Marianne Bascomb. Mebbe yore foolin' yorself. Anyways, I figgered it out, sittin' here, that a man's got a right to do what he thinks is best. Good luck to yuh.'

Sabin walked up the path to the parade ground. He looked toward Officers' Row. The Bascomb quarters were well lit up. *He* was probably there. Sabin stopped and lit a cigar. He had learned plenty about Frank Grayson Khuyper since the column had left Fort MacNaughton.

Khuyper had been a law student in 1861, and in 1862 he had enlisted in the Kansas Militia, rising swiftly to the rank of first sergeant. In 1863, Jim Lane of Kansas had used his influence to have a second lieutenant's commission presented to Khuyper. By the fall of 1864, Khuyper sported the twin bars of a captain without having seen any more action than a skirmish against some guerillas at Harneyville. The only spot of glory on his record was the defeat and capture of Shay's Independent Frontier Company on the Badwater, with Shay's Company almost out of ammunition and badly cut up after defeating a large band of raiding Kiowas.

The war was almost over. Too much rank and not enough glory had rubbed off on Frank G. Khuyper. The rumor around the post was that Khuyper planned to make his home in Oregon after the war. With a brevet commission and an honorable war record he would be in solid with the Union men of the new territory. A beautiful, gracious wife, with money of course, would shine beside Frank Khuyper as he began the long climb to political heights. The study of law was almost essential for political prominence. That . . . and money. Colonel Clay Bascomb had plenty of that last item.

Sabin strolled toward the big barracks where the dance was being held. He stepped up on the porch and leaned against a post. Every window held its little group of lonely enlisted men watching the fortunates inside. Their eyes studied each woman, thin or fat, plain or pretty as though each one was a goddess temporarily visiting earth to ease the harsh burden of frontier duty for a pitifully short spell.

Sabin looked over the clumps of heads at

the nearest window. Katherine Williams was dancing with Stacy Bascomb. She wore a dress he had never seen before. She was far prettier than he had ever realized, and her eyes were all for Stacy Bascomb. Then Sabin stiffened, taking the cigar from his mouth. Naturally he recognized the tall, broad-shouldered officer standing on the sidelines, near the sweating orchestra. Frank Khuyper. But it was the woman beside him, standing with white-gloved hand resting possessively on Khuyper's arm, who riveted Sabin's attention. It was *her*. She looked like an exquisite Dresden figure.

Sabin devoured her with his eyes. She was like a bird of paradise compared to the other women in the hall. Sabin walked to the door, kept open because of the heat in the place. He walked in and took off his forage cap. He stared steadily across the crowded floor. Suddenly she saw him.

Sabin placed his cap on a hook and skirted the crowd. He came up behind the couple. Khuyper did not see him. 'May I have the honor of the next dance, Miss Bascomb?' Sabin asked with a bow.

Khuyper whirled. Hot blood rushed up beneath his fine skin. 'Shay,' he said, 'you're on detail.'

'I was, sir. Finished a few minutes ago.'

Khuyper seemed almost ready to strike. 'Miss Bascomb is here with an officer, Shay.'

Sabin smiled. 'I know, sir. Nice of you to honor the enlisted men's dance. Very nice indeed, Captain Khuyper, sir.'

Sabin had him then, and Khuyper knew it. Sabin took Marianne as the next dance started. Halfway across the floor she glanced back at the raging captain.

'Sabin,' she said. 'He hates you. Why did you do this tonight?'

He grinned. 'It's the privilege of any enlisted man, isn't it? One of the few times in his miserable life when he can dance with the chosen few. Besides, we're leaving tomorrow. I had to see you.'

'Why? We may never see each other again.'

'We're both moving west.'

She looked away. 'They say the Indians are gathering in great strength along the trail. Colonel Collins refuses to give Father permission to leave until things are safer. Sabin, it's *so* dangerous out there.'

A side door was right beside them. Before she knew what he intended, he swung her out on the wide side porch. The porch was deserted. He drew her close and kissed her. She pushed him back. 'Sabin! You're mad! He's insanely jealous!'

He raised his head. 'He's *insane*. I'll agree to that. How can you associate with a madman like that?'

She bit her lip. 'There's so much pressure on me. From Frank. From my Father. Even from Stacy. I seem to be some kind of chattel. Father seems to think I should marry Frank. Frank plans to settle in Oregon after the war. Father says it will protect our future there.'

Sabin felt cold all over. 'That man is responsible for the death of my brother. Many of my men died in filth and neglect because of him. Some of them were shot down in cold blood. Why? Because he was wounded at the Badwater. Because we fought them to the last cartridge. Any honorable man would have forgiven us that last hard fight. But not *him*! It was a personal affront to his ego. He'll never be satisfied until he sees to it that every last one of us Galvanized Yankees is killed off. One way or another.'

'Take me back,' she pleaded. 'I don't know what to do, Sabin. *Before God, I don't know what to do!*'

He gave it up. They walked back inside. 'Thank you for the dance, Miss Bascomb,' he said, and bowed. As he walked away he could feel the cold shaft of Khuyper's eyes boring into the back of his neck. The odd thought came to him that Marianne Bascomb would some day wake up to the fact that she had married a monster. Too late, of course. Then she could do one of three things. Leave him. Kill him. Or do what her mother had done in years gone by when *she* realized what kind of man she had married. Somehow Sabin knew it would be the last. God help Marianne

123

Bascomb.

Katherine Williams stood near the front door of the hall, smiling at a red-faced corporal. Sabin stopped in back of the non-com. 'This dance is mine, corporal,' he said.

The corporal seemed almost relieved as he walked away. Sabin bowed formally. 'I'm sorry,' he said. 'I was placed on extra fatigue. Did Giddings tell you?'

She nodded.

He looked down at her pretty gown. 'I've never seen that before,' he said.

She blushed a little. 'I was helping Miss Bascomb. Stacy asked me to attend the dance with him. She insisted I wear this.'

'Where is the gallant Stacy?'

She nodded across the teeming floor. 'At the punch bowl.'

'Stacy likes his liquor.'

'Oh, be quiet!' she snapped.

Sabin grinned. 'Look, Kathy. I'm sorry about the whole thing.'

She frowned fiercely at him. 'So? Is that why you went to *her* first like a bee after pollen? Simpering and smiling? Sometimes you make me sick, Sabin Shay.'

'Sometimes I make *myself* sick, Miss Williams.'

She looked away and then laughed. 'Somehow I can't really get mad at you. There are times when you look so stern and angry, then suddenly you seem able to play the fool without much effort.'

'A neat picture of my whole life,' he said with a sigh.

Stacy Bascomb skirted the edge of the crowd with two brimming punch glasses in his fine slim hands. His face reddened when he saw Sabin. 'What are *you* doing here?' he blurted.

Sabin ignored him. 'This is our dance, Katherine,' he said.

'Please,' she whispered. 'I need the work from Miss Bascomb. *Please*, Sabin. Don't make trouble.'

Sabin stepped aside. Stacy smirked. The kid was half drunk already. Sabin walked outside and felt for a cigar. It had been a damn fool stunt to rile Khuyper.

Sabin saw Warner Giddings leaning against a post. The light from the hall glittered on the rows of braid festooning his narrow chest. He grinned at Sabin. 'Through for the night?' he said.

'Yes.'

Giddings nodded. 'I got a bottle of forty-rod,' he said, 'and I ain't about to hog it myself. I'd admire to have yuh help me kill it, Cap'n Shay.'

Sabin smiled. 'Never let a comrade down yet,' he said. He took Giddings by the arm. 'Where does the execution take place?'

'In the tent. Ole Howell sent me up to see

how yuh was.'

'Well, thank you.'

'I looked in and seen yuh with Miss Bascomb and then with Miss Williams, Cap'n Shay. Two purtiest gals at the stompin'. How do yuh do it?'

Sabin grinned. 'Easy,' he said. 'I just grab an earring and stick it in my pocket. Then they have to follow me around.'

They ambled down the graveled pathway. Giddings glanced back at the brightly lit hall. 'Quite a difference between them two fillies,' he said, and neighed like a small, pleased horse. 'Yore a lucky man in some ways, Cap'n Shay.'

'How so?'

'I never seen Miss Bascomb look at that skunk Khuyper like she does at you, nor I never seen Miss Williams look at that Bascomb brat the way she does at you.'

Sabin placed an arm around Warner Giddings' thin shoulders.

'Boy,' he said solemnly, 'after the war is over, Shay's Independent Frontier Company will live again. By God, we'll form us a reunion-type marching and drinking club for holiday parades and such. And when that glorious day comes, remind me to promote you to corporal.'

Giddings tilted his head. 'Shore will. You really think that day will come, Cap'n Shay?'

Sabin increased his pace. 'Certainly. Let's

get that bottle. I feel like I've got a heap of drinking to do before dawn.'

They had a heap of drinking to do before spring, it turned out. Not that it changed anything, or anybody. Every human being on the post seemed to be frozen into his own set role throughout a winter that would never end.

But winter did end. Spring came early to Wyoming that year. Summer arrived in a rush. And the troops took to the field...

CHAPTER FOURTEEN

Fort Laramie lay over one hundred and fifty dusty miles behind Donaldson's command. Far to the north, tall nimbi towered over the dim hills. Eerie sheet lightning played across the clouds scarring them brightly.

Sabin Shay drew rein on a rise ahead of the slow-moving column. The supply wagons bounced and joggled in the ruts of the road. The dust threading up from the mules and horses hung over the sweating infantrymen who slogged ahead of the wagons. One cavalry company led the column, while another closed up the rear, eating the dust. Now and then the vagrant wind tattered the dust and brought the sound of rumbling wheels and thudding hoofs to Sabin.

For two days there had been no Indian sign. No lone warrior sitting his paint horse on an elevation watching the passage of the column on the Great Medicine Road. There had hardly been a day on the long journey where at least a dozen warriors had been seen eyeing the Mila Hanska, the Long Knives, as they slogged along. But there had been no slashing raids by the Crazy Dogs, Dog Soldiers and Stronghearts.

Sabin rode on. A mile ahead of him he could see Cobb Howell and Uh-sah-wuck, Spotted Horse of the Pawnees, watering their horses at a buffalo wallow. Far on the northern flank of the column other cavalry scouts were paired up with Pawnees. Ames Lockerby and Si Webster were out there somewhere.

He joined Howell at the wallow. 'Just look at this buffalo tea,' Howell growled.

The water was brown, and an odor of ammonia rose from it. Sabin shook his canteen. 'I'll do without it,' he said. 'Never could figure out how a buffalo can stand in water, peeing and crapping into it while he's drinking it.'

Spotted Horse was a thick-bodied man, wearing a cast-off issue undershirt hanging over his breechclout. His moccasins were worn thin. His hair was roached and from it depended a single feather. He looked like a typical Fort Laramie 'ration Injun,' but he

128

was a warrior of some standing in his home village of Arikararikuchu. He was a member of the Two Lances, entitled to wear the black moccasins during ceremonial occasions, for he had consecrated the buffalo four times.

Cobb jerked his head at the Pawnee. 'Gabby, ain't he?'

Sabin chuckled. He nodded at the Pawnee. 'How does it go, brother?'

Spotted Horse glanced at the lightning-riven clouds. 'No good. Voice of Great Spirit. No good.'

'You have seen the enemy?'

'No Cha-ra-rat.'

'What the hell is he saying?' Howell asked.

'No enemy.'

'Time to look for 'em is when you don't see 'em.' Cobb took out three cigars. 'Last of my stock from the sutler. Light up, Cap'n Shay.'

Sabin and Cobb lit up, but the Pawnee stuffed the dry tobacco into his mouth and munched on it.

'Look at that,' the big trooper said.

Sabin drew the smoke into his lungs. 'Few Pawnees can smoke. They have to qualify in some ceremony.'

'Queer ducks.'

'Matter of opinion. We whites have some queer notions ourselves.'

Howell stood up and pointed east. 'Column's gainin'. You want to wait and report?'

129

'Hell no!'

Howell shoved back his forage cap and wiped the sweat from his face. 'Khuyper been rawhidin' you again?'

'Naturally.'

Cobb Howell rubbed his hand against his holster. 'First gunfight we get into with them Sioux, I'm hopin' Khuyper gets in my way.'

'You may have to get in line, Cobb.'

They mounted and rode west, followed by Spotted Horse. The Pawnee's eyes moved constantly, studying the terrain. Three miles from the buffalo wallow he kneed his mouse-colored mare close to Sabin. He thrust out an arm, pointing down a long slope toward the sluggish coil of the river.

'What's up?' asked Howell.

Sabin looked west. Beyond a loop of the river he saw a group of buildings set back from the road. 'That must be Sage Springs Station.'

'Sho! That's where we're headin' ain't it?'

Sabin nodded. 'It's called Fort Bowen now.'

Cobb scowled out across the great shallow bowl of country, ringed by low hills, with ridges of naked rock like dislocated bones, thrusting themselves through the shallow soil. 'Hell of a place. Nothing but sky and hills. Every Dog Soldier in Wyoming can sit on them hills an' look down into your mess tin to see what you're eatin'.'

130

Sabin relit the stub of his cigar. 'I don't like the looks of this place. See those hills near the ford? A natural place to ambush anyone traveling the road.'

They rode down the slope, eyeing the hills. A coyote loped through the brush and vanished into a draw. A thread of smoke drifted up from the old stage station to stain the clear sky. The wind had shifted, bringing a breath of cool air from the north where the nimbi brooded over the mountains.

Spotted Horse half-cocked and capped his rifle. He shifted his lance sling from his right to his left shoulder.

'Take a look into those hills,' Sabin said.

The Pawnee kicked his heels against the sides of his horse and rode north of the road to circle in on the hills. Antelope jacks rose up out of the brush and raced away from the Pawnee.

'How many men the Yankees got in that station?' Cobb Howell asked.

'About a platoon.'

'Infantry?'

'Cavalry.'

'That so? Where's the hosses?'

Then Sabin knew what had been bothering him. The big corral, set off to one side of the station and back from the main buildings, was as empty as last night's bottle of rotgut.

They left the road and flanked it a half mile to the south. The dust rose from the grass.

Spotted Horse was out of sight.

An icy finger of loneliness seemed to trace a wavering line down Sabin's sweaty back. An air of brooding hung over the shallow valley, as though it was hiding some dark secret.

They drew rein a quarter of a mile from the river. The Pawnee came out of the hills, riding swiftly. He held up something as he neared the two white men. It was an ankle-height moccasin. He gave it to Sabin. Sabin examined it. 'Sioux,' he said quietly.

'Cha-ra-rat,' Spotted Horse agreed.

'How the hell do you know it's Sioux?' Howell asked.

'Lazy stitch. Isoceles and right-angled triangles. See how they've been combined into hour-glasses, diamonds and two-pronged forks? The Cheyenne designs are similar.'

Cobb nodded. 'There's dried blood on that skin fringe at the heel.'

Sabin looked at the little fort across the river. There was still no sign of life. The bastards must be asleep. The three scouts rode toward the ford.

The wind shifted, blowing from the fort.

'My God,' Cobb Howell said.

The wind had brought a sweetish rotten smell to them. The wind-borne horror was sending them a silent message. Howell's horse shied and blew at the edge of the water. There was something in the shallows. Something covered in greenish blue cloth. A dead soldier, the bloated body taut against the soaked cloth.

Spotted Horse kneed his horse away from the two white men as the corpse seemed to move. The pent-up body gas was forcing itself out. The foul stench drifted to the two white scouts.

Howell stood up in his stirrups. 'Look,' he said. 'In the eddy. Three more of 'em.'

Sabin turned to the Pawnee. 'Stay here,' he said. He knew damned well it was a useless thing to say, because the Pawnee wouldn't go near that silent fort.

The two white men rode across the ford and drew rein a hundred yards from Fort Bowen. The doors were closed and the windows shuttered. The tendril of smoke still drifted from the huge rock chimney. The odor of death thickened about the two scouts.

Sabin unsnapped his carbine swivel and capped the Sharps. Howell followed his example. They touched spurs to their horses. They encircled the fort. There was no sign of life. The wind banged a loose shutter and Sabin's nerves jumped.

Sabin slid from his horse. 'Stay here, Cobb,' he said.

'With pleasure. I'll cover yuh.'

The last fifty feet to the front door seemed an eternity to Sabin. He shoved at the thick door with his carbine butt. It swung open on creaking hinges. Then the full blast of the charnel house hit him. He gagged and turned away. He slipped his scarf up over his nose and mouth, took a deep breath of fresh air, and walked into the big common room of the station.

Men were scattered about the floor like bundles of bloody rags. A pipe-ax protruded from the back of a sergeant's head. A corporal lay near the door with his feet and right hand hacked off. Arrows bristled from every body. Sabin felt a sour flood well up in his throat. He crossed the stinking room. A man lay near the fireplace, but his body wasn't swollen tight against his clothing. He lay on his back near the smoldering fire. Bits of a broken ammunition box were half-burned in the fire. Sabin knelt and touched the dead man's face. It was still warm. The poor bastard had been severely wounded and his hands were twisted in the blood-soaked undershirt. He had evidently lived there for several days in that rotten tomb, unable to move, feeding the fire as a silent message to whoever might come near the station.

Sabin counted ten dead men in the big room and four others in a smaller room. The Sioux had gone through the station like beer through an open bung. He came out of the back door. Cobb Howell beckoned to him. He pointed out a mass of horse tracks behind the corral in a soft area near the walled springs. 'Musta been about a hundred of 'em,' he said. 'How was it in there?'

Sabin pulled his scarf from his face. 'Like the Alamo after Santa Ana got through with it.'

'Wonder how it happened?'

'*Quien sabe?* They might have got careless. The Sioux may have broken in at dawn and got every damned one of them, even those that broke for the river bottoms.'

Blue-clad horsemen topped the ridge across the river. They drew rein. The setting sun flashed on fieldglasses as an officer studied the fort. Spotted Horse had ridden along the river and was swimming his horse across. He came out of the river and rode his dripping horse in tight little circles, pointing to the hills behind the fort.

Sabin whirled. There were warbonneted warriors against the sky line. Over a hundred of them. Laughing at the stupid Mila Hanska below them. They had taught the Long Knives a lesson. Then to the west and the north, other horsemen appeared. Cheyennes, Sioux and Arapahoes.

Cobb Howell looked at the advance guard of the column. He began to sing.

'Come home, John,
Don't stay long.
Come home soon
To your own Chick-a-biddy.'

The advance came swiftly down the hill. A

135

trumpeter's mount shifted into an easy singlefoot to ease the trumpeting. The clear notes of the C horn filed across the valley. Then the first company showed up on the ridge.

The hostiles watched the Long Knives until they reached the river. Then they vanished as quickly as they had appeared.

Howell wiped the nervous sweat from his face. 'It's as hot as a Dutch oven with the biscuits burnin',' he said.

The advance threw up sheets of water tinted bloody by the dying sun. The bloated corpses bobbed in the miniature waves.

Sabin waited for Lieutenant Teale. He saluted. 'Mr. Teale,' he said, 'the garrison has been wiped out. Four bodies in the river. Fourteen in the station.'

Teale paled. 'No survivors?'

'We haven't found any, sir.'

The troopers shifted in their saddles as the fetid stench drifted to them through the open door. They looked nervously at each other and then at the hills where a wraith of dust marked the passing of the hostiles. They felt like Christian martyrs in a great natural Coliseum, with the blood-hungry eyes of two hundred hostiles glaring down at them.

Teale dismounted and eased his crotch. 'Was the spring fouled?'

Cobb Howell nodded. 'Two dead mules in it.'

Teale turned. 'Sergeant Carmody! Haul the mules out of the spring. Finch! Ride back to Major Donaldson and tell him what's happened. He'd better jump up some dust getting down to the river. We don't know where the hostiles are.'

Finch spurred toward the river. Teale walked to the door and poked his head in. Suddenly he turned and spewed a sour flood out on the ground. 'Oh, Lord,' he spluttered. 'That's Jim Hartnett in there with his men. Jimmy and I enlisted back in Kansas three years ago.'

The sun was almost behind the hazy hills as the column wound down to the river and crossed it. Troopers of the advance had looped picket lines about the feet of the dead men and had hauled them out into a hollow beyond the station. Most of them lost the beans and bacon from their last meal before they finished the job.

When the sun went down the wind carried the shrieking laugh of a coyote down to the nervous men at Fort Bowen. Then the cry was repeated from hill to hill, so that they knew they were ringed by a great circle of the finest natural horsemen in the world, patiently waiting another chance to cut the Mila Hanskas to bloody ribbons and send them across the Shadow Waters.

CHAPTER FIFTEEN

They had buried the eighteen bloated dead in the neglected post cemetery. The buildings had been scrubbed and disinfected. But the aroma of death still clung stubbornly as though to remind the living that death was always close.

Major Donaldson sent out patrols with orders to go no farther than the first line of hills. Too many men had ridden over the hills in that country to vanish from sight forever, or to be found in undignified death, slashed and mutilated. The telegraph line was still out, although Corporal Kerr tested his key every hour. The hostiles had been clever enough not to touch the line within sight of the post, hoping that some of the Long Knives would ride over the eastern hills to trace the break. The post itself was safe enough. The hostiles knew better than to ride into the fire of Walk-A-Heaps sheltered behind log walls. They wanted the slow-riding horse soldiers to come out after them.

There was no news from the east, and the garrison had no knowledge of what was going on farther along the line. Perhaps there was nothing but a string of charred station ruins with blackened corpses silently garrisoning

138

them.

The post flag snapped in the strong wind every day, reminding the soldiers that this was indeed an outpost of the United States, but to all appearances, they might have been the first men on a silent, manacing planet, thousands of miles from Mother Earth.

A quiet new enemy showed its scabby head at Fort Bowen. One by one, men fell prey to fever, aches and nosebleeds. Rashes and rose spots appeared on their abdomens. Hamish Hume diagnosed it as typhoid.

Sabin waited outside the small hospital one day for news of Charlie Kester.

Hume wiped the sweat from his face with one hand as he felt for a cigar with the other. 'Typhoid,' he said. 'Charlie's tough. It's the major I'm worried about. He's had a relapse. Hemorrhages.'

'That leads to—'

'Yes.'

'We can't afford to lose him. If Khuyper gets in the saddle there will be pure hell to pay around here.'

'I've heard that he wants to send out a patrol to find that break in the telegraph.'

Sabin spat. 'You know why. The bastard is dying to get a message from Marianne Bascomb.'

Hume raised his eyebrows. 'It's gone that far?'

'You know damned well it has! He'd

sacrifice good men to get that line through just to hear from her.'

'I've asked for you as temporary medical orderly.'

'Thanks,' Sabin said dryly.

Hume grinned. 'You're welcome. Fennessey got into the medical alcohol last night. Man, but he was fighting drunk!'

'He's regretting it. Khuyper has him lashed to a wagon wheel out in the sun.'

'I'll stop that. The man won't live.'

'Here's your chance. Here comes Khuyper now.' Sabin snapped to attention as Khuyper stopped in front of Hume.

Khuyper stared at Sabin. 'Have you no duties?'

'I was on guard last night, sir. The second night in a row—sir.'

'Captain Khuyper,' Hume said quietly, 'the typhoid may spread. It may have been caused by water that was used five to fourteen days ago. Typhoid usually requires a minimum of five days after infection for the fever to start.'

'What are you doing about it? We can't afford to have men lying about in hospital, Hume.'

Hume flushed. 'Treatment requires careful nursing. All excreta must be destroyed. I'll need screening of some sort for my patients. I believe the flies spread the disease.'

Khuyper laughed. '*More* of your fine

theories.'

Hume raised his head. 'I don't tell you how to screen an infantry column with cavalry, nor how to establish Cossack posts. Please don't question my theories as a medical man!'

Khuyper shrugged. 'You'll have to do the best you can with what you have.'

'I'd like to have Trooper Shay detailed as a medical orderly to replace Fennessey.'

Khuyper glanced suspiciously at Sabin. 'Why?'

There was a dryness in the Scot's tone as he answered. 'He had good opportunity to learn his business at Fort MacNaughton, you may remember.'

Khuyper's mouth drew into a tight line. 'I'm in command here. The man has been assigned as a scout. I may have need of him very soon.'

'For what purpose?'

'An eastern patrol, Hume. I want that telegraph line repaired. For all we know the war may be over.' The cold eyes flicked over Sabin's set face. 'I'd like to hear of Lee's surrender.' Khuyper wanted Sabin to rise to the bait. He had plenty of wagon wheels exposed to the blazing sun.

Hume looked east toward the hazy hills. 'A dangerous business, Frank.'

'Soldiering is always dangerous business,' Khuyper said, as though *he* had seen plenty of danger while in uniform.

Hume rubbed his lean jaw. 'The major will not allow any such patrol.'

Khuyper smoothed down the front of his blouse. 'Will he recover, do you think?'

Hume looked again at the plum-colored hills. 'You might as well know now as later. I do not think so.'

Khuyper straightened. 'Too bad. Keep me posted, Hume. I've got to get this garrison better organized while I have the time.' He strode away, vastly pleased with himself.

Hume rubbed his hands on his trousers as though to rid them of something unclean. 'Bloody swine,' he said.

Sabin nodded. 'He's like a buzzard floating low over something that's dying, waiting for his chance.'

'I hope to God Donaldson recovers. If he doesn't, Sabin, Khuyper will sign your death warrant by sending you over those hills.' Hume relit his cigar and closed his eyes as if weighing a decision. 'There is a way,' he said softly.

'What do you mean?'

'The nights are dark. Khuyper pokes about the post at all hours. The hostiles are close in at night.'

Sabin shook his head. 'The time will come for me to kill him, Hamish. But I want him to *know* who killed him.'

* * *

Sam Donaldson died shortly after the notes of Retreat died amongst the shadowed hills. Twenty-five hard years of wearing the blue. Top man of the Class of 1840. He had lived through the tornado at Punta Rasa in 1841 as junior officer of the old Eighth Infantry, when Camp Caloosahatche had been obliterated. He had participated in the battles of Palo Alto, Matamoras, Monterey and Buena Vista under Taylor in the Mexican War. Later he had transferred to the dragoons and served at half a dozen different frontiers posts. In '61 he had been wounded at Wilson's Creek, as a captain of cavalry. In '63 he had been promoted to major and brevetted lieutenant-colonel. His army account was now closed: *'Donaldson, S. M., Major—from Duty to Died of Disease.'*

The Army is an old institution. The old Regulars are wise in the ways of officers. In time some of that sage wisdom rubs off on the Volunteers. Some of the men had liked Donaldson; others had disliked him. But every one of them had respected him. There is a difference. Now Sam Donaldson had gone and Frank Khuyper had taken his place. A subtle demoralization seemed to hover about the fort. For none of the men liked Khuyper.

Furthermore all of the men knew his record. There was no question of his personal courage. Let him kill himself in a wild dash for glory against the waiting hostiles. But Frank Khuyper had proved once before that he could and would take other men to die needlessly with him. And Khuyper wanted a brevet. He had no chance of getting it against the Rebels now, but there were Indians aplenty. A man could shoot for record and glory out in Wyoming almost any day of the week. The rumor in the sanitary sinks of isolated Fort Bowen was that Frank Khuyper wouldn't waste much time in his search for the strumpet Glory.

One hour after evening mess on the day Sam Donaldson died, Sabin Shay stood booted and spurred with Troopers Phin Harris, Aaron Fitch, Ames Lockerby, Ben Carver, Harry Banning and Jonas West. Spotted Horse stood by his mouse-colored mare. Harris, Fitch and Lockerby were former members of Sabin's company. Carver, Banning and West were a poor selection of the Kansas Volunteer Cavalry. With the exceptions of Lockerby and Spotted Horse, they were not men with whom Sabin wanted to face a circling ring of Sioux and Cheyenne horsemen.

Khuyper came from his quarters and stamped his feet on the hard earth as though enjoying life to the fullest. He drew in deep lungfuls of the fresh air, and then he looked at Sabin. 'You're in charge, Shay,' he said.

144

'West is a former telegraph operator for the railroad. You have your tools and key, West?'

'Yes, sir,' West said sourly.

'Good. I want that line in. Understand?'

'How far shall we go?' Sabin asked.

Khuyper folded his arms and cupped his chin in his left hand as he looked at the eastern hills, almost as though some spirit was communing with him. 'Two days at the most. No dawdling! Don't think you can hide in the hills and kill time, and then come crawling back here saying you can't find the break.'

Sabin said nothing. He saluted and left before the temptation to say too much overcame him.

The patrol crossed the dark river, followed by the eyes of the men in the picket post. 'I'll bet we won't see them boys again,' said a lean private. 'How come Khuyper puts a Galvanized Yankee in charge?'

A corporal spat a stream of tobacco juice into the river. 'That's easy. He hates his guts. I heard a sanitary sink rumor at Fort Laramie that Shay used to spark that Bascomb filly. Even before that, though, Khuyper hated his guts. Shay and his men were prisoners at MacNaughton. They say Khuyper was responsible for Shay's brother dying there. I don't like Rebels, Harry, but I'm damned if I ain't on Shay's side.'

Harry nodded. 'Khuyper's a brassbound sonofabitch. I sure ain't looking forward to serving under him. Things weren't so bad with Donaldson in command.'

'Uh-uh.' The corporal yawned. 'But you forgot one thing, Harry.'

'What's that?'

'The Sioux, Cheyennes and Arapahoes up in them hills. They ain't going to make it easy for *anyone* out here.'

The patrol rode up into the dark hills. There was no talking. Just the creak of girths, squeak of saddle leather and the soft thud of hoofs in deep dust.

On the ridge, Sabin looked back at the yellow lights of the fort. Khuyper had worked things out pretty well. He had to admit it. If the patrol survived, they'd mend the break in the line so Khuyper could hear from his light-o'-love. If they didn't survive, Khuyper would be rid of Sabin Shay.

I'll come back, Sabin told himself. I'll come back and see *him* dead.

He wished he believed it.

CHAPTER SIXTEEN

A girth-high mist shrouded the shallow creek. Sabin shivered in his one blanket. It was almost dawn, and they had bivouacked beside the creek an hour ago, chewed cold cooked rations and fed their horses with good oats

146

from the nosebags. The wind moaned faintly through the creek bottoms and whined about the telegraph line. They had found no break. Sabin planned to stay hidden during the day and ride on after dark.

Sabin stood up and walked about the area. Carver, one of the two guards, was asleep with his back against a tree. Phin Harris, the other guard, was shivering under his blanket. He said, 'I don't feel well, Cap'n Shay.'

'You're in good company,' Sabin told him.

Sabin circled through the little camp. He glanced at Fitch's blankets. Then he strode over to them. They had been filled with heaps of long grass. Sabin went to the horses. One of them was missing. Fitch had pulled foot. Sabin walked to the edge of the creek and listened. No sound of hoofbeats penetrated the windy darkness beyond the camp.

Spotted Horse materialized like a ghost.

'Fitch is gone,' Sabin said.

'No hear anything.'

'Scout along the creek.'

Spotted Horse disappeared into the darkness. He was back in twenty minutes. 'Horse tracks in mud. Man ride southeast. Fast.'

Sabin nodded. He hoped Fitch had enough sense to hole up during daylight.

The dawn filled the eastern sky with cold light. Sabin walked up out of the bottoms and looked east out over the rolling plains. Ames

147

Lockerby came up behind him. 'Yuh see him, sir?'

Sabin shook his head.

'He's loco. Them hostiles will pick him up.'

'I know. To hell with him. It's the rest of us I'm thinking about.'

'Spotted Horse is along the bottoms. Phin Harris says he's sick.'

'He usually is.'

They stood there for a long time, talking aimlessly to ease the strain. The sun came up. Suddenly Sabin caught the odor of wood smoke. A thread of bluish smoke drifted up above the low trees. Sabin cursed and plunged down the slope, and through the shallow creek. Banning, Carver and West were squatting about a fire. Sabin shoved West aside and kicked out the fire.

'What the hell is the matter with you?' West yelled.

'You fools! Every damned hostile in the hills may have seen that smoke!'

'We was only going to make coffee,' Carver said.

Banning hiccupped. 'Damn Rebel thinks he's a corpril or somethin'. I say we're Union men. We ain't about to take orders from no damned Galvanized Yank.'

Lockerby cocked his Sharps. 'Get up, you bastards.'

Sabin looked up at the sky. The smoke was

148

drifting with the morning wind. 'Boots and Saddles,' he said, 'We'll head south along the bottoms and then come out in those low hills.'

West stood up. 'I say we go back to Fort Bowen.'

'Shut up,' Lockerby said.

West flexed his muscles and shoved Sabin. 'I ain't saddling no horse. I'm heading back.'

Sabin hit him with a short right and knocked him over the embers of the fire. 'Get up,' he said softly. 'Get up or I'll break your jaw with my foot.'

West got up and held his jaw. 'I ain't forgetting this,' he said.

They led the horses up the creek, splashing through the shallow waters. Two miles from the bivouac they met Spotted Horse. He pointed south 'Cha-ra-rat. Chase Fitch. No good.'

Sabin slogged up the rise. He saw specks far out on the plain. Six of them. One ahead and five behind. Dust threaded up behind them. He couldn't distinguish Fitch, but he knew the Pawnee was right. As he watched, Fitch's horse went down and then the five specks closed in on the speck on the ground. Aaron Fitch would never see San Antone again.

'Now what?' Lockerby called.

'I say we go back!' West yelled.

'Through them hills?' Phin Harris said. He

149

wiped cold sweat from his narrow face.

Sabin mentally cursed Frank Khuyper, Aaron Fitch and the three stupid Yankees who had started the fire. He led his horse up the creek and halted where the trees thinned. Indians knew better than to camp in creek bottoms, but they also knew it was a habit of the white men. The hills he had planned to hide in were two miles across an undulating plain. There was scant cover, but they'd have to risk it.

Lockerby covered the three Kansans with his Sharps. They led their horses out into the open. The wind rippled the short grass. Banning took a drag at his canteen. The men looked up at the low hills. They felt naked. It was a hell of a big country and a long way from the walls of Fort Bowen.

Sabin and Spotted Horse dropped back. They were two hundred yards behind the others when it happened. It didn't seem quite real. The thin line of horsemen shot out of a hidden draw like a shaft driven by a one hundred pound bow. Indians, Sioux. Stripped to gee strings, covers stripped from their war shields, feathers rippling with the speed of their motion. The rising sun shone on the brass trim of carbines and rifles.

Banning turned greenish white. West swung up on his mount and spurred it toward the creek. Carver fumbled with his carbine sling. Lockerby hooked his reins over his left arm and cocked his carbine.

There was death in the swift advance. Painted and feathered death, sweeping down in a long arc to cut between the two small parties of Long Knives.

Phin Harris screamed. He dropped his carbine and ran away from his horse. He ran straight toward the mouth of a draw to the west. He ran full on into a group of warriors. A muzzle-loader spat a chewed slug into his chest. With hardly a change in gait, a burly warrior sank a pipe-ax into Harris' skull as the little man pitched forward. The warrior swung down, whipped out his knife, neatly circumscribed the narrow skull and ripped off the reeking scalp. Then he straightened up on his pinto and raced after his mates.

The two sickles cut in on the three troopers. Carver went down with a shaft driven into his breastbone. Banning turned his face away from sure death and retched out a sour flood of liquor and food. A lance drove in behind his left shoulder blade, smashed him down, and jerked free, dripping blood.

Lockerby got off one shot. He whipped out his Colt and dropped a claybank. The rider hit the ground running and caught a ride behind one of his mates with hardly a change in pace. Then the dust swirled about Ames Lockerby as he fought alone. His Colt spat four more times. The hostiles drew off, circling like a great wheel, with only a leg and arm showing over the tops of their lathered mounts. Lockerby shook his free fist at them and then jammed his pistol muzzle into his mouth. The report was muffled as he blew the top from his head.

Sabin drew his Colt and shot his bay. Spotted Horse killed his mouse-colored mare. They dropped behind the quivering bodies. Sabin thrust his Sharps forward, raised the sight and fired. The big slug drove a buck from his horse.

Spotted Horse fired and slowly reloaded. He looked at Sabin. 'No good. Uh-sah-wuck knew all time. Gods angry.'

The Pawnee stripped to his gee string. He slapped his chest as he eyed the enemy. The hostiles had drawn off. Wet scalps dribbled blood down the sides of their lathered ponies. West had made the creek and was nowhere in sight.

Sabin wet his lips. Twenty of them sitting their ponies out there. There wasn't a chance now. Fear spread a green mucus over his mind. His guts tightened and then relaxed.

The dead men lay like bloody rag bundles under the sun. Their faces had loosened like watery pie dough. The hostiles swung away from the dead and circled widely. Sabin fired his Sharps and missed. He cursed as he lowered the breech and slid in another cartridge. He'd have to settle down. This was for the record.

Spotted Horse fired. A pony buckjumped and shot out of the circling line. His rider jumped clear as the pony went down.

A warbonneted Sioux shook his shield four times toward heaven. '*Co-oco-o!* Get ready!'

Then the first charge came like a bolt straight from hell, almost up to the two men lying behind the dead horses, only to split and race away, with the hostiles hanging onto the far side of their ponies. Sabin had wounded a buck while Spotted Horse had dropped another pony. It was good strategy, for Indians of the Plains hated to fight afoot.

Three warriors drew off to one side. One of them was barrel-chested, with strong bowed legs which clung to the barrel of his horse like thick clinging vines. There was something vaguely familiar about him. He was a warrior of proven standing. There could be no doubt about that. And he was talking war—big war. He had enough of foolishness. The trio rode back to their mates.

Sabin wet his lips. Sweat soaked into the thick wool of his uniform. 'No reserve and no support,' he said to himself.

Spotted Horse did not look at him. The Pawnee seemed to know he was going to die. Like all primitive minds, he was still open to the whisperings of the fates.

Three times the glory charge came, led by the stocky warrior Sabin had singled out. Three times the charges split. Two warriors

153

were down, one of them dead, the other thrashing about with a shattered leg. The hostiles drew off. This was getting serious. Too many men had been lost. The two behind the bullet-pocked horses must die.

For the fourth time the screeching warriors came in. Sabin heard a sound like that of a stick being whipped into thick mud. Spotted Horse grunted. He fingered the bluish hole below his left ribs, eyeing the flow of blood. He squinted at the dust-shrouded horsemen and then cut a ten-foot length from his issue picket line. Slowly and deliberately he tied it about his lean waist and then to the haft of his lance. He coughed. Blood trickled from his mouth. He slapped his chest as he stood up.

'I go,' he said thickly.

Spotted Horse carefully stepped over his mare and walked fifty feet toward the watching warriors. He thrust his lance into the ground, leaning heavily on it as he did so. Then he slapped his chest and stood there defiantly with his knife in his left hand and his Colt in his right.

Sabin reloaded. The Pawnee was doomed and so was he.

The charge came like a freshet. Spotted Horse emptied his Colt as calmly as if he were on the range. Then he sank down on one knee, still facing the enemy. Blood flowed from a scalp wound, half-blinding him. He began his death song.

The enemy call came clearly on the wind. '*Co-oco-o!* Get ready!'

Sabin fired as they came on. There was a spume of dust and a splattering of foam as the warriors drew up in front of the lone Pawnee. Forehooves thrashed as the ponies flung off. A warrior drew back the string of a horn bow. The loosed shaft struck Spotted Horse full in the center of the forehead, quivering with vibration. The barrel-chested warrior hooked his bow over one arm and flung his lariat. The loop settled about the neck of Spotted Horse, jerking him off his feet. The Pawnee was dragged, bouncing and jerking, behind the horse of the man who had killed him. Another warrior had snatched the coveted lance from the earth.

The sun beat down mercilessly as the hostiles gathered out of range. Sabin Shay looked at them from under the vizor of his slanted forage cap. The long road was ending. He felt curiously calm now. He had seemed to know all along that the patrol would be wiped out. Spotted Horse had accepted it by his way of death. *A man of men, Spotted Horse.* A man could always die like a man.

He sweated there for an hour while the warriors squatted in the shade of their ponies. There was no hurry. They would get him. One Mila Hanska, lying behind two swelling horses, eyeing the others who had died. It was good to let him wait and think about the manner of his death.

There was one amongst the warriors who sat alone, watching the white man behind the horses. He did not move very much, that big soldier. The warrior hoped he was not dying. In the last wild charge the warrior had looked full into the sweating face of the white man, and had known who he was. Wakan Tanka had at last brought back the white man who had wronged him. It was good. He stood up. '*Co-oco-o*,' he said in his deep voice.

Sabin raised his head. A dull ache had begun to thud across his temples. His vision swam a little as he watched the warriors. They mounted and began riding slowly toward him. He braced himself. Time for one carbine shot and five from the revolving pistol. The last slug was for himself and to hell with posterity.

Then they burst into swift action, racing down on him. One warrior didn't make it. A fifty slug smashed his chest. A Colt slug smashed a brown arm. The rest closed in shrieking their courage word. '*H'gun! H'gun! H'gun! H'gun!*'

Sabin stood up to die.

Four more shots blasted out of the Colt before a lance ripped across his arm and a lathered pony knocked him to one side. The Colt was gone. He snatched up his Sharps and reversed it. Three warriors slid from their sweating mounts to count coup by touching him. One of them went down with a smashed shoulder. He knocked the second cold. The third was a barrel-chested buck with a face as hard as flint. He ducked under a swing of the Sharps, touched Sabin with his left hand, screaming for a count of coup. Then as he swung up the warclub, he shrieked his name twice for Sabin to know.

'Mato Najin! Mato Najin! Standing Bear! Standing Bear!'

The last thing Sabin remembered was the glancing blow of the warclub and the rush of greasy bodies bearing him down on the bloody grass. A rifle butt thudded behind his ear and he collapsed into a bottomless vortex that whirled him around and around, giddily, until he went into the little death of unconsciousness.

The sweating warriors waited for Mato Najin to strike the death blow. Standing Bear stepped back.

'No,' he said huskily. 'This Long Knife is for the little torture fires. I have spoken.'

A pock-marked warrior frowned. 'He went down like a man,' he said.

Standing Bear slid his hand down to his knife. 'I say he lives long enough to scream under the little torture fires. Do you question me, Lame Deer?'

Lame Deer hesitated. Some said that Mato Najin was sick in the head. He was a great warrior and a great horse thief, but something

157

in his eyes did not seem right. Lame Deer shrugged and stepped back.

Standing Bear felt the blood wash through his brain. It was always so after a hard fight. This one had been harder than he had expected. But there were many others of the white soldiers in the little fort to the west. More coups and more scalps. Glory for Mato Najin. Now Wakan Tanka had rewarded a favored son by placing in his hands the white man who had stolen Pretty Hands from him so many colds ago. It was good. *Everything* was good. It was the time of war.

CHAPTER SEVENTEEN

Sabin opened his eyes to look up at a lowering sky. An oxhide drum seemed to be beating at the base of his splitting skull. He turned his head a little, cautiously fingering the bloody hump behind his left ear, and saw a young buck squatting nearby with a Sharps across his naked thighs. The guard tried not to show his curiosity in the big white man, but it was hard to conceal.

The rest of the warriors were acting like kids, ripping through the pile of bloody clothing and equipment they had gathered from the broken bodies of the dead. Sabin wet his gummy lips with his tongue.

158

'What will they do with me, brother?' he ventured in rusty Cheyenne.

Blank surprise showed on the broad face of the young buck. 'You speak the language of the Dzi-tsii-tsa, Long Knife?'

'It is so. You are of The People. Yet most of the others are of the Seven Council Fires.'

'It is so. They are of the Border People. Those Who Camp By Themselves.'

Sabin remembered now. They had fought like the Hunkpapas, the grimmest of the mighty Sioux Nation. He said, 'That is Standing Bear who leads?'

The Cheyenne nodded proudly. He shifted the Sharps so that the muzzle centered on Sabin. The big Long Knife had fought like two bears.

'How is it that you speak the tongue of The People?' he asked.

'Many colds ago,' Sabin said, 'I lived with the band of Little Eagle.'

The warrior tilted his head to one side. 'But you are a Long Knife! An enemy!'

'*Hou!*'

'Maheo was good to us today,' the buck said.

Sabin glanced at the bloody wreckage of his patrol. Maheo had indeed favored the Sioux. 'How are you called?' he asked.

'Swift Runner.'

The first fat drops of rain struck the dusty earth. Sabin struggled upright as the warriors

159

swung up on their ponies and lashed them toward him. Standing Bear was heavier than Sabin remembered him. A warrior now of many coups. In the old days there had been a sullenness about him coupled with an air of uncertainty. Now it was gone. Standing Bear had a hard face, the face of a fighting sub-chief. Pride, endurance, cruelty and experience had etched themselves deep—and also, contempt for Sabin showed very plainly.

'Dog,' Standing Bear said. 'White dog. I have waited long.'

Sabin spat deliberately to one side. 'Give me a knife, Loud Talker,' he said. 'Face me and fight.'

The chief spat full into Sabin's face. Two warriors slid from their mounts and hustled him over to Ames Lockerby's horse. They practically threw him up on it, swiftly lashing his ankles together under the barrel of the horse. Sabin felt the saliva run down his cheek. He closed his fists as they lashed his wrists together, and an odd thought struck him. Frank Khuyper and Standing Bear resembled each other in no physical respect whatever, yet they were alike under the skin. Khuyper had done well. He had delivered Sabin Shay into the hands of his Indian blood brother.

★   ★   ★

Hours later the warriors topped a ridge and hammered down a long slope, throwing gobs of mud from the hoofs of their ponies. The rain had increased steadily all day. Sabin's crotch felt as if it might split any moment. There had been no food or water for him, although the warriors had gnawed at *wasna* while they rode.

In the bottoms, along a sluggish creek, there were at least fifty lodges. The smoke drifted from the smoke holes and hung like a thick scarf amongst the cottonwoods and willows. Many ponies were herded in a meadow across the rain-stippled creek. Paints, palominos, spotted grays, mouse blues, buckskins, bayo coyotes, dun coyotes and pure whites.

The raiders flourished their fine new weapons and scalps coated with drying blood. They slid from their wet ponies as the people gathered about them. A pock-marked warrior cut Sabin's ankles loose.

'*Mani! Mani! Walk! Walk!*' the pock-faced warrior barked.

Sabin felt lonely as a hawk as he walked through the pressing crowd. A stone glanced from his shoulder. A squaw spat in his face. Pock-face shoved him into a sagging teepee. He sat down beside the cold ashes of the firehole. He had nothing to look forward to except the 'little torture fires' which would be kindled at his staked-out hands and feet and allowed to move up as his extremities burned away. The Women's Society would pour hot fat on his flesh and force him to drink bowls of urine. They were worse than the men.

Sabin peeked through the flap. The camp was mixed. Sioux, Cheyenne and Arapahoe. A warrior stood guard at the front of the tent. The rain pattered steadily and leaked through the smoke vent.

A cold wind swept through the bottoms, billowing the sagging teepees. The warriors were all under cover, being cared for by their womenfolk. Sabin was safe for the night at least. He lay down on a tattered buffalo robe and went to sleep.

★   ★   ★

A hard hand shook him awake. He blinked in the dim light. A fire was flickering into life in the firehole. He stared at the hatchet face which hovered over him. 'Little Eagle,' he said quietly.

'It has been many colds since you have been in the country of The People, Lone Hunter.'

'I have traveled. I have been to war, my brother.'

Little Eagle squatted beside Sabin. 'Maheo has frowned on The People. It is *emeoestove*—the time of war here also. The Seven Council Fires mean to close the Big

Medicine Road. Here there are many Dzi-tsii-tsa, O'ho-omo-io and Hi-na-nae-inan, ready for war.'

Cheyenne, Sioux and Arapahoe, thought Sabin. 'You do not like the thought of war, my brother?'

'It is so. I am an old man. I have few ponies left. Once I was a Crazy Dog, with many coups. Now I am an old man whose voice is weak in council. But the Hunkpapas pray to their Big Holy and the Thunder Music of the Hi-na-nae-inan is heard always in the hills. The Long Knives travel the Big Medicine Road. It is not good.'

Sabin rubbed his numb wrists against his chest. 'You have not forgotten how we hunted the buffalo, my brother? How we shared the good hump meat? Have you forgotten?'

Little Eagle's eyes were pools of melancholy in the light of the quickening fire. He bowed his head. 'That was many colds ago. Standing Bear never forgot you. He is leader here now.'

Sabin held out his hands.

Little Eagle looked away. 'There are many strong voices here. They feel their power. They have stopped travel on the Big Medicine Road. They have captured many fine weapons from the Long Knives. The young men cry for war and the newly risen chiefs will lead them to drive the Long Knives from this

163

land.'

'You have not said you will help me, my brother.'

Little Eagle stood up. He dropped a piece of wasna onto the robe. 'It is in the hands of Maheo. Good-bye, Lone Hunter.'

A great loneliness settled upon Sabin. There was no expression on the lined face of the old chief. 'I am an old man,' Little Eagle said as he paused by the door flap. 'My two strong sons have gone to the Land of Shadows. There is nothing left for me in life. You were like a son to me, Lone Hunter.'

'It is so, Little Eagle.'

'I do not want to see you die like a dog for the cooking pots.'

A faint spark of hope grew in Sabin. Then Little Eagle was gone. Sabin gnawed at the pemmican the old man had left. The rain sluiced down steadily. The warriors would stay close to their fires, leaning against their backrests, playing the moccasin game. If the rain died out during the night, the next day would be the last on earth for Sabin Shay.

CHAPTER EIGHTEEN

The Thunder People were in fine fettle. A vicious rain slashed at the lodges while lances of lightning shot through the night and forked into the buttes. The creek began to roar as the waters rose steadily.

Sabin's guard came into the teepee and crouched near the door, praying in a low voice. The Blue Cloud People were brave in battle but deathly afraid of nature's manifestations.

'Maheo is angry,' Sabin ventured. 'He will wash away *hesec*, the blessed mother soil.'

Rivulets of water were trickling across the lodge floor. One of them hissed into the firepit, raising steam.

'Maheo is angry,' Sabin persisted, 'because The People have dared to raid the Big Medicine Road and cut the talking wires.'

Thunder rumbled in the hills. Lightning shot across the streaming sky. The rivulets coiled like snakes across the lodge floor. The Cheyenne eyed them. The Long Knife had said Maheo might wash away the blessed mother soil.

Lightning flashed and snapped angrily close to the lodge. The odor of the discharge filled the air. The Cheyenne fled from the lodge and vanished into the night.

Sabin rolled up on his knees and then to his feet. The thongs about his wrists were too strong to break or loosen. He peered from the teepee. The village street was thick with mud. There was no one in sight. Sabin lay on his back and propelled himself through the greasy mud by thrusting with his heels. The creek roared by close to the lodges. Sabin hunched his shoes against a tree and worked himself up to his feet. The horses were beyond the creek, huddled against a low bluff.

Sabin worked his way into the rushing waters, swaying as the current tore at him. He did not see the blanketed figure which followed him from the village. Ten feet from the far shore he went under, rolling over and over with the force of the current. Panic shot through him as he fought on the greasy bottom to get on his feet. His lungs were ready to burst and his senses reeled. Then his hand reached the surface long enough for him to draw in a deep breath. He crashed his shoulder against a fallen tree and started to go under again. Then something twined in his thick hair. It pulled hard and hurt like hell. He yelled, filling his mouth with water.

Then he was up on his feet again, plowing through the thick bottom mud, following the punishing pull on his hair, until he floundered out of the water. He fell over a rock and sprawled face downward in the cold mud, drawing air deep into his chest. Then his wrist bounds suddenly gave way. They fell loose as if cut. He looked up at the blanket-shrouded figure which stood over him. 'Who are you, my brother?'

There was no answer.

'Little Eagle?' asked Sabin. The figure was

too slight for that of the old chief.

The eerie lightning shot across the sky. Then the mysterious hooded figure suddenly threw back the flap of blanket which concealed its face.

'For the love of God!' Sabin said.

There was no mistaking her. Pretty Hands. Older, but even more attractive with her added years. The lightning faded away, leaving them together in the streaming darkness. Sabin lurched to his feet, rubbing his swollen wrists, not knowing what to say or do.

'Come,' she said quietly. She led the way through the trees. Half a mile from the camp she led him into a brush-shielded cave which cut deep into a sheer bluff facing the rushing creek. She gripped his hand with her small wet hand and led him on in the ebony darkness with a sureness which showed that she had been there many times before. She made a hard right turn. She released his hand. He stood there in the blackness. Then she struck a light and lit a torch which jutted from a cleft in the wall. She gazed at him with liquid eyes.

Sabin drew her close. She did not resist. He felt her full unhampered breasts against his wet chest. He raised her face and kissed her. But there was no response. The old fire was gone. She pressed him back with the slim lovely hands which had given her her name.

167

'I saw you, Lone Hunter,' she said, 'as they brought you into the village.'

Shadowed sadness softened her face. Sabin reached for her but she drew back.

Why did you never come back?' she asked.

There was no use in lying. The simple directness of Pretty Hands had always disarmed him before. *'Emeoestove,'* he said. 'The time of war came for my people.'

'The white man's war began four colds ago,' she said gently.

She had him there. He had left her in the spring of '58. Sabin glanced back toward the cave entrance and then at the flickering torch. 'I've got to get out of here,' he said.

'I know. Standing Bear has it in his heart to hear you scream like a white woman.'

'I'll need a horse and a gun.'

She nodded. She did not move.

Sabin slapped a hand against the damp cave wall. 'Well!' he snapped. 'I *meant* to come back! There were many day's journeys between us! The war started!'

Her liquid eyes held his. 'You could have taken me with you,' she said.

Sabin leaned back against the wall. His nerves were fraying. The massacre of his patrol. The shock of being captured by the Indian who hated his guts. The certainty of a death by torture. His life being saved by Pretty Hands. It had unsettled him so that he wasn't sure he could go on. There was just one thing he did know—he *had* to get out of here fast.

She came close to him. 'You will take me with you now?'

'Yes! Yes!' he said. 'Only hurry!'

She came closer to him and slid her arms about his neck, drawing his head down. Her lips sought his in the way he had taught her to kiss him in the days long ago when she had been a naive girl. Sabin kissed her. She snuggled close and the cold realization came to him that she expected to be loved, then and there, as proof that he really wanted her to go with him.

Thunder thudded in the skies. Sabin placed his hands on her shoulders and gently pushed her back. 'The People will be looking for me,' he said swiftly. 'There is no time, Pretty Hands.'

She clenched her little fists. He hadn't fooled her a damned bit. But she turned and walked from the cave. Sabin put on a dry, greasy shirt he found in the back of the cave along with a miscellaneous pile of junk. The only weapon the junk pile yielded was a short bar of rusted iron. He doused the torch. He felt his way to the mouth of the cave and waited there, listening to the thrashing of the brush.

He leaned against the wall of the cave, debating whether or not he should take off through the woods on foot and to hell with

169

help from his former squaw. Yet he was too beat to get far without a mount. He'd have to wait for her.

There was a darting movement. He barely caught it in the corner of his eye. He whirled, raising the iron bar, but it was too late. A squat, barrel-chested buck held a huge revolver inches from Sabin's gut. The lightning revealed the pitiless face of Standing Bear.

Sabin dropped the bar into the mud. The lightning flickered away, leaving the two of them standing there in the streaming darkness. Sabin's stomach drew up into an icy ball. Damn the girl! Her delaying had allowed the sub-chief to find him.

Standing Bear shifted. 'Turn,' he said.

Sabin turned, feeling the pistol muzzle press at the base of his spine. There was a chance the revolver might be too wet to fire, but it was too long a chance. The odds were that Standing Bear would march him back to the village. The sonofabitch wanted him to die slowly. Maybe he should make a break. It would be better to die with a bullet through the back than from the little torture fires.

The muzzle pressed harder and then Standing Bear fell heavily against Sabin. Sabin whirled in time to see Pretty Hands standing over the fallen chief.

'He is not dead,' she said. She held up a heavy Savage revolver and touched the barrel with a slim forefinger. Sabin drew her close. There were no horses in sight. She gripped him by the slack of his shirt and led him through the darkness to where a blocky gray stood with hanging head.

Sabin took the Savage from her hands and slid it inside his shirt. He stood there, not knowing what to say.

Pretty Hands motioned toward the camp. 'The People are to gather here,' she said. 'There will be at least five hundred warriors. The Big Medicine Road is to be closed forever by the warriors of Standing Bear.'

Sabin considered going back to the cave. His hands gripped tighter. It would be easy to get rid of Standing Bear right now.

The thunder almost drowned out her voice as she spoke again. 'Do not fear that I will go with you, Lone Hunter. My heart tells me you are not the same man who shared my lodge many colds ago.'

He could not think of a thing to say that would make sense.

'Good-bye, Lone Hunter,' she said.

He bent to kiss her, but she fled into the wet woods like a startled deer. He swung up on the gray. 'Pretty Hands!' he called. The wind tore the words from his mouth and scattered them into meaningless fragments of sound. The Thunder People chuckled as they drove their great arrows of lightning across the tumultuous skies.

Sabin headed west, upstream, riding by instinct. Far behind him, Pretty Hands padded softly back toward camp. She walked with her head down, listening to the tiny squishes of water in her moccasins, thinking the little thoughts that held away the big sadness. Standing Bear had not seen her. He had known she would take her white man to the cave, but he had not seen her and he could not prove a thing. She smiled bitterly into the black night. Standing Bear would not speak even if he could prove that she had helped Lone Hunter to escape. Not with that lump on his head. Not when The People would know that she preferred Lone Hunter as her lover.

She was safe. She was alone again. She walked on, softly, toes turned slightly in, Indian fashion. And as Indian women had done since The People came to exist, she cried silently, dry-eyed, letting the tears run down her throat, so that not even the trees could see.

CHAPTER NINETEEN

Sabin Shay came out of the hills at dawn, a gaunt lath of a man, riding an exhausted horse. Smoke drifted up from Fort Bowen. Sabin's breath caught in his throat. Among the many wagons there, he could distinguish the fancy Dearborn in which Marianne Bascomb lived on the trail.

He led the bay to the ford and rode it across. A corporal raised his rifle as he stepped out of the little picket station. He said, 'Hand over the pistol, Shay.'

Sabin cocked a curious eyebrow at him. 'What's up?'

'Get that pistol, Josh,' the non-com said over his shoulder to a private.

Sabin handed over the clumsy Savage. 'What is this?'

'West got back alive. Said you led the patrol into a trap and then deserted.'

'He's a damned liar!'

'Maybe. But we got orders to arrest you on sight. You're in a mess, man.'

'I've been in a mess ever since I took the oath.'

'That figures. You could have avoided that too.'

'How so?'

The burly non-com smiled leisurely. 'Taken the oath of allegiance to the Old Flag back in '61,' he said.

He marched Sabin into the headquarters room. Khuyper sat at his desk. Sergeant Schmidt looked up from the eternal paper work of a topkick long enough to warn Sabin with his eyes.

Khuyper leaned back in his chair. 'Now I

173

suppose I'll get some cheap heroic story of escape from bloodthirsty hostiles.'

'Not from me, sir.'

'Where were you?'

'The hostiles jumped us ten miles or so east of here. Lockerby, Fitch, Banning, Carver and Spotted Horse were killed. I was captured.'

'West claims you led the men deliberately into a trap and then deserted.'

'He's lying.'

Khuyper swiveled his chair and glanced through the window. He spoke over his shoulder. 'Donaldson was too soft with you and the rest of the Rebel scum. I'm going to make an example of you, Shay.'

'I'm entitled to a hearing.'

Khuyper whirled and smashed a hand flat down on his desk. 'You're entitled to absolutely nothing! This is war! The penalty for desertion is the firing squad. You deny that?'

Sabin shifted. The guard half-cocked his rifle.

Khuyper thrust out an accusing finger. 'You'll be bucked and gagged until such time as I decide your penalty.'

'There are regulations, sir. I'm innocent until proven guilty—'

Khuyper stood up. 'Get this through your thick Rebel skull. *I'm* the regulations here. We'll see how easily you talk after a few days of gagging!'

Sabin was marched to the improvised guardhouse. They walked past one of the outbuildings. Marianne Bascomb sat in a chair while Katherine Williams brushed the beautiful blonde hair. Katherine glanced at Sabin, gasped, started to speak, and then didn't. Stacy Bascomb lolled on a cot beyond her, grinning.

They tied Sabin's wrists and ankles together. They forced his lashed wrists down in front of his knees and thrust a stick over his left forearm, under his knees and over his right forearm. A trooper said, 'Open your mouth, Shay,' and then he looked at his mate. 'God, but I hate to do this to a man, Martin.'

'Go ahead,' Sabin said.

Martin swore. 'It's been hell around this outpost of Hades ever since that Bascomb doxie got here and got Khuyper in heat.'

They closed the door behind them. Sabin eased his back against the wall. He tried not to think. The thing he needed now was sleep.

★　　★　　★

The cell was dark when Sabin heard the rattling of the bolt. A lean figure crossed to Sabin and placed a plate and cup on the floor. The man lit a candle stub. Sabin looked into the gaunt face of Kinston Forbes. 'That sonofabitch,' the Texan said.

Forbes untied Sabin. Sabin pulled the soaked gag from his mouth.

'The boys are ready to break,' Forbes said in a low voice.

'No!'

Forbes squatted beside Sabin and spooned food into his mouth while Sabin worked his stiffened muscles. 'There's a score of us, countin' you, Cap'n Shay. Ain't no hostiles kin cut *us* down if we fight like Texicans.'

'The hills are crawling with them.'

'They don't fight at night. We figger we kin break out of here after midnight, get hosses and make for the hills. Comes daylight we kin hole up and ride on after dusk.'

'To where?'

'West, o' course. Mebbe we kin—'

'No, Forbes! It's not time.'

'Look, Cap'n Shay! Khuyper's been ridin' hell outn' us Galvanized Yankees. Burial details. Loadin' details. Latrine diggin'. Extra guard duty. Hellfire! He even had some of us clean out the cabin thet Bascomb filly lives in. To top it off, so help me, we had to dig a privy for her special use. We got us a bellyfull.'

Sabin drank deeply. 'I say it isn't time.'

Forbes grunted. 'Yore first rate in our book, Cap'n Shay, but we sorta knowed yuh wouldn't go fer the plan. So we formed a committee. Me, Charlie Kester, Cobb Howell and George Fletcher. We aim to go, and we aim to take yuh with us.'

'Let me talk to your committee first.'

'All right. I'll get the boys to come here.'

'Dammit, no! Khuyper will gag and buck the lot of you!'

Forbes chuckled. '*Him?* Hell! He's dinin' with thet Bascomb filly tonight. He don't see nothin' but her figger and them come-to-bed-with-me eyes of hern. These Yank guards is all right. The Yanks hate Khuyper about as much as we do. Three of 'em went over the hill the night yuh went out on patrol.'

After Forbes left the cell, Sabin paced back and forth. The guard looked in now and then but made no effort to see that Sabin was bucked and gagged again. It seemed Forbes was right about the feeling of the Yankees against Khuyper.

The conspirators showed up shortly before Tattoo. A bottle passed from Cobb Howell to the guard. He cached it under a loose board along the eaves and then unlocked the cell door.

'How are yuh?' Howell asked.

'About beat,' Sabin said.

'We can't figger how yuh made it back here.'

'I'll tell you the whole story some other time. Right now I want to talk against this break.'

177

Kester pulled at his lower lip. 'Things have gone from bad to worse. Bascomb and the emigrants had a rough time. Lost six waggins near Sandy Crossing. One of them was Katherine Williams'. Seven emigrants and four soldiers were killed. The waggins was supposed to stay at the Platte Crossing, but Bascomb had his way—as usual.'

'Tomorrow afternoon,' Howell put in, 'some of us has orders to cut firewood along the crick. We aim to steal food and cache it out there. We kin take care of the guards tomorrow night and light out on the hosses.'

'Supposing the alert goes out?' Sabin asked.

'We'll git us a passel of Yankees as well as the hosses,' Fletcher said.

'Fools,' Sabin said angrily. 'Can't you wait until the hostiles pull foot? They're sitting up there waiting for any movement from the fort. Be patient, can't you? No Indian was ever born who'd sit out a siege like a white man. If there's no easy loot for the taking, they'll wander off. Let's wait.'

'We ain't!' Kester snapped. 'We stay here much longer and someone will kill Khuyper.'

Howell leaned against the wall. 'Maybe the cap'n is right. We're a hulluva long ways from safety out there.'

'It ain't goin' to git any safer,' Fletcher protested.

Sabin played his last card. 'Maybe
178

Khuyper will let the wagon train proceed. Maybe we'll be ordered to go with it. Our chances would be better.'

'Fine chance of him doin' thet,' Fletcher said.

'He knows we're the best Indian fighters he has. He isn't about to let Marianne Bascomb go on without giving her the best protection he can.'

Kester nodded slowly. 'That makes sense. I got to admit it.'

George Fletcher sighed. 'I'll agree to wait a few days. But that's all.'

Howell walked to the door. 'Three days is the time limit. No more.'

Kester waited behind the others. He gripped Sabin by the shoulder. 'When that young woman got here all she did was ask about you and then looked up into them damned hills.'

'Marianne?'

'*Her?*' Kester spat. 'Lordy, no! I mean the Williams gal.' He walked out into the darkness.

CHAPTER TWENTY

Khuyper's threats against Sabin never materialized. Without explanation, on the second day, Sabin was released and told to report to Sergeant Schmidt.

Schmidt eyed Sabin's swollen wrists. 'Godt verdamnt! Sometimes I think this Khuyper shouldt haff been in the Prussian army yedt. There, such treadtment iss expected!'

'You don't like it, Sergeant Schmidt?'

Schmidt slapped a big hand down on his packing crate desk with such force that a nail popped out. 'No! I servdt mine time in the old country as a boy. Lashes ve godt. Breadt und vater ve got. Like dogs ve vere treadted. It iss nodt goodt to treadt soldiers like dogs. Soldiers are men!'

'Thanks,' Sabin said dryly.

Schmidt grunted. 'Wass it nodt for the lady, Shay, you vouldt still be in the guardhouse yedt.'

'Miss Williams?'

'Der liddle vun? No. The vun midt yellow hair.'

'You mean Miss Bascomb?'

'Ja. She leads Khuyper aroundt like a liddle dog on a chain. Such a fool he iss for that voman.'

'What happens to me now, sergeant?'

Schmidt leaned back in his chair. 'Der hills iss still ful midt Sioux. Many uv der men are sick midt typhoid. I godt to make out duty rosters midt nodt enough men to do it midt. A sergeant-major's job I godt midt first-sergeant's pay.'

'It's the old army game, Schmidt.'

'Ja! I tell Khuyper ve needt scoudts to see what dem Sioux iss going to do. Maybe that iss vhy he ledts you oudt.'

'I see. Maybe I was better off in the cell.'

'Gedt cleaned up. Repordt for duty.'

Sabin got stiffly to his feet. The sergeant jabbed a thick finger at him. 'Shay! Don'dt you gedt any ideas on going over der hill. You gedt caught and you vish you'dt never been born!'

Sabin walked outside. It was a clear day. The rains had washed the skies and the heat had not yet formed a haze on the sharply outlined hills. Sam Nelson, the emigrant wagonmaster, was checking the wheels of a Conestoga.

'Glad to see yuh out,' Nelson said.

'Gracias.'

'Damn fools,' Nelson grumbled. 'I told these bastardly emigrants to put three inch tires on their wagons back at Westport Landing. We got enough wedges in some of these tires to raise Chimney Rock. Sand gets in 'em and works 'em loose.'

'How long do you figure on staying here?'

'The ground is still soft. But it will be all right in a day or two. But movin' is out.'

'How so?'

Nelson spat a streamer of amber. 'Reason is that moon-eyed Khuyper is sparkin' that Bascomb female.'

'The hills are full of hostiles, Sam.'

Nelson shrugged. 'We got plenty good riflemen. If Khuyper gives us some cavalry we kin make it. O' course we'll have losses, but these Pukes and Suckers is anxious to git to Oregon and they're willin' to pay the fiddler's fee to git thar. Trouble is, that Bascomb has better waggins and better animiles. I kin only move as fast as my slowest waggin. Bascomb kin make miles to my yards with his rollin' gear. He's been workin' on Khuyper to let him go on with a strong cavalry escort.'

'And the hell with the emigrants.'

'Yeh.'

'So you'll sit here a while.'

Nelson scratched in his beard. 'Supplies is low. I figgered we might get by on buffler out thar. Ain't seen any. Guess the hostiles druv 'em off.'

'I didn't see any. Just buffalo skull circles.'

Nelson nodded. 'The hostiles figger the Big Holy will bring back the buffler if they make them circles.'

Sabin rubbed his wrists. 'Time is running short. Khuyper will either have to let you go or turn you back to Laramie.'

'The hell he'll turn us back! I aim to talk to him and that stuck-up Bascomb bastard. There'll be hell to pay once I get 'em together.'

Sabin went on to his tent. Warner Giddings was dozing on his blankets. Sabin cleaned up and then drew a set of arms and equipment from the quartermaster. He folded the Lone Star guidon in the bottom of his haversack. Almost five months has passed since it had snapped in the breeze. He had made himself a rash promise about it, just before he left Fort MacNaughton. Now he wondered if it would ever fly again, even as a nostalgic symbol.

★   ★   ★

Uneasiness hung like a pall over little Fort Bowen. The telegraph line was still out. Now that Marianne was with him, Khuyper made no effort to get it repaired. Fort Bowen was a good setup for Frank Khuyper. He had two companies of cavalry and a company of infantry, along with a small detail of quartermaster and medical service men. He was in complete charge of his little world, and except for the menacing tribesmen in the hills, it was a good world. He drank of Colonel Bascomb's liberal supply of bourbon and smoked his inexhaustible clear Havanas. And to top it all off, Marianne Bascomb seemed to have accepted his suit.

Khuyper was alone in his happiness and confidence. The other officers knew a showdown would soon be due. Of the hundred and twenty-five troops at the crowded post, a fifth were in the hospital. Sam Nelson worried himself sick. Some of his wagons were in bad shape. His draft animals were not allowed quartermaster forage but must be pastured along the river under a skeleton guard of troopers and emigrants.

Typhoid had struck amongst the emigrants. Two children had died and a score of the adults were prostrated with it. Khuyper had the emigrant wagons moved behind the station in a motte of cottonwoods to quarantine the civilians from post limits. But, paradoxically, he allowed the Bascomb wagons to remain on the post proper, and issued forage to Bascomb for his draft animals.

Sabin came off herd guard at midnight the day of his release. Lamplight showed in Khuyper's room. Sabin glanced through the window. Khuyper was playing poker with Colonel Bascomb, Stacy, and Lieutenant Teale. A bottle stood on the table and blue tobacco smoke rifted in the drafty air.

A low light was burning in Marianne Bascomb's quarters. As Sabin passed he heard a low voice call his name. He stopped and saw her standing in the shadows wrapped in a dark cloak.

'What is it, Marianne?'

'Are you all right, Sabin?'

'As well as can be expected, I reckon.'

'No one expected to see you come back, Sabin.'

'It was close,' he admitted.

184

Jasmine drifted to him. 'I'm afraid,' she said. 'I want to leave this terrible place. The odor of death seems to be everywhere. Yet I'm afraid to leave.'

'It's one or the other, Marianne. A bitter choice.'

'The typhoid is gaining, Surgeon Hume says.'

'You're safe enough.'

'Father is afraid of Asiatic cholera. He says it would spread like wildfire through the post.'

'There are no symptoms of it.'

'Many people have died of it on the trail.'

Sabin waved a hand. 'The Oregon Trail is no pleasure jaunt.'

She seemed to want to talk with him. She leaned back against the wall, letting her cloak swing open, revealing a filmy nightgown. A sort of sickness grew deep inside of Sabin. He suddenly realized how long ago it had been since he had had a woman. Marianne was a real piece of feminine goods.

She placed a hand on his forearm. 'They say you know this country better than any other man here.'

'Yes.'

She came close. 'Couldn't you take me away from here? We could ride at night. They say the Indians won't fight at night. You could get me through, Sabin.'

'What of your father and Stacy? What of

Frank?'

'They don't seem to be too concerned about my well-being!'

'And I should be?'

She rested her head against his shoulder. The pungent odor of spirits mingled with the jasmine and suddenly he knew why she wanted him. 'Have you forgotten *everything?*' she asked.

'No.'

'Then come in. I want to talk with you.'

'I'm on the ragged edge around here. I can't take chances.'

She looked up at him and smiled.

'You either come, Sabin, or I'll scream. You know what Frank would do to you. I talked him into releasing you. One scream and he'll have you shot.'

She was so damned skilful in getting her way. Sabin followed her into the dimly lit room. There were two cots in it. One of them covered with silk, the other with coarse trail blankets. Katherine wasn't there, but Sabin knew she had been staying with Marianne.

Marianne shut the door and placed her back against it. 'She's with those filthy emigrants,' she said. 'Nursing. If Father knew he'd discharge her. He pays her well to help me.'

'Nice of him,' Sabin said dryly.

'You didn't expect me to live without help?'

186

'No, Marianne. I'm surprised you get along with *one* maid. How many did you have in New Orleans? Five or six?'

'Oh, shut up! I don't seem to know you any more.'

The air was thick with the mingled odors of perfume, women, and oddly, liquor. He picked up a slim bottle. 'Vermouth,' he said.

She filled two glasses. 'It helps my nerves.'

Sabin sipped the liquor. He had heard often enough that her mother had been a heavy drinker. Absinthe. She had taken to the wormwood distillation after she learned that the colonel had a quadroon mistress. In time Therese Bascomb's mind had become deranged. Delirium and idiocy had followed.

Marianne downed two drinks quickly. 'Will you take me?' she asked again.

'I'm in the Yankee army now.'

'I'll forgive that. I don't know how you had the stomach to take the oath, but it doesn't really matter. The war is almost over. I forgive you, Sabin.'

He walked to the door. 'The last damned thing I want from you, Marianne, is forgiveness.'

She gripped his left arm with surprising strength. 'Damn you! You always were so high and mighty! Yet you took advantage of me when I was a mere girl!'

'I took—' Sabin couldn't help but laugh. 'How many were ahead of me?'

She slapped his face with her free hand. Sabin gripped her wrists. 'Listen,' he said quietly. 'You got into this mess with that sanctimonious father and puling brother of yours. Now get yourself out of it.'

Tears filled her eyes. She pressed against him. 'God, Sabin! Help me! I don't know what to do!'

'You've got Frank Khuyper.'

'Damn him! Damn my father! Damn Oregon!'

She dragged on his arm, pulling him with her, pulling him down atop of her as she fell loosely on Katherine's bed. He felt her full warm body through the thin gown. She wrapped her arms about his neck and pulled him close, thrusting her body up against his in a paroxysm of released passion. The liquor-wet lips mashed against his. The old desire swept over him, and then suddenly cold reason gripped the bridle reins and hauled back on the bit. He started to get up. She ripped the gown from her full breasts.

The door opened. Sabin broke away from the thrashing woman beneath him. He turned to look into the taut face of Katherine Williams. Marianne sat up and laughed at her. 'You see?' she asked. 'He's just like all the rest of them!'

Katherine closed the door. 'Get out of here, Sabin Shay,' she said. 'You're in enough trouble as it is.'

'Get out of here yourself,' Marianne said thickly.

Katherine reached for the door handle but she kept on looking steadily at Sabin.

'Please,' she said.

Marianne laughed. 'I've seen Stacy pawing *you*.' She stood up, swaying back and forth. She reached out and plucked at the shabby dress. 'Look at you,' she said. 'God alone knows what Stacy sees in you.'

Katherine pushed Marianne's shaking hand away. 'Maybe he sees a lady,' she said quietly.

The Southern woman swayed and passed a hand across her eyes. 'I—' She staggered slightly. 'I feel sick.'

'Please go,' Katherine said to Sabin Shay. 'Unless you want to see her in worse condition than she is.'

Sabin shrugged. 'Why don't you get out of here?' he asked. 'Go back to the wagons.'

She shook her head. 'No. They've given me work here. I have no way to get to Oregon alone.' Her eyes held his. 'You never really loved her, did you, Sabin?'

Marianne had dropped onto the bed. She beat steadily with small fists against the blankets. 'Oh God,' she whimpered. 'I want to go home. I want to go home.'

Sabin opened the door. Katherine came out with him. 'I'm sorry for her,' she said.

Sabin tipped her piquant face. He kissed

189

her lightly. 'You can forgive anything from anybody,' he said.

She turned away. 'Don't be too sure about that.' She closed the door behind her.

Sabin did not see Matt Duggan watching them. Nor did he see the big man walk swiftly toward Khuyper's quarters.

CHAPTER TWENTY-ONE

The white worms writhed in Stacy Bascomb's gut that morning after his drinking bout with Frank Khuyper. He felt deathly sick, but he knew he must kill Sabin Shay. What had started out as a boredom-dispelling dalliance with Katherine Williams somehow had developed into a powerful desire for the independent Missouri girl. Like all his kind, Stacy needed a strong and vital woman as a leaning post through life. She was poor but she was as different from the gaunt, slatternly Puke and Sucker women as a blood filly differs from a draft colt.

Stacy had been protected throughout his useless life by his father's position and wealth. His mother had left him in the care of a faithful, pampering mulatto nurse. Marianne had always showed spirit and determination, but Stacy, as he grew older, developed a taste for bourbon, cards, quadroons and octoroons, with a pure black now and then to vary the course. He had inherited his mother's taste for liquor and his father's craving for women, and to give Stacy *some* credit, he damned near outdid the old man. The one thing he had not inherited from either side of his family, nor shared with his sister, was a leavening of fighting spirit. In short, he had a yellow streak down his back as wide as his narrow shoulders.

Stacy Bascomb had inherited *one* thing from his father: an ability to scheme his way through life letting others do the dirty work. Matt Duggan was a tool fashioned to fit Stacy's hands. Duggan, rough and ignorant, with a half-mad light in his muddy green eyes. Built with a muscular and bone structure that could give him the edge in a bloody rough-and-tumble, groin-kneeing, eye-gouging battle. It would be easier to pay for a simple knife thrust in Sabin Shay's back, but Stacy wanted to see the bloody wreckage of the man who had slapped his face at Fort Laramie, the man who now had the inner track with Katherine Williams.

The trick would be to arrange for Matt to get at Sabin in some isolated, secluded place. There would be a way. Trust Stacy Bascomb to find that way.

*   *   *

A sickly moon lit the eastern sky. It was quiet about Fort Bowen. Entirely too quiet. Sabin came off guard to find a note pinned on his bunk. It was from one of the emigrant women, and it stated that Katherine Williams had suddenly taken ill and wanted to see him. She was at the wagons, in the quarantine area.

Sabin left the tent, thrusting his Colt beneath his belt. He passed through the motte of cottonwoods. A sentry clumped along the western edge of the motte. Otherwise the place seemed...

Something moved behind Sabin. Something hard pressed into the small of his back.

'Walk over toward the crick,' said a familiar voice. 'Don't get no funny ideas of makin' no break, Shay.'

The pistol jabbed hard into Sabin's kidney.

'Walk,' Matt Duggan said.

After they were screened by brush and trees, near the river, Duggan stopped. Two dismantled emigrant wagons stood to one side. 'Throw that Colt into the bresh,' Duggan said.

Sabin disarmed himself and turned.

'Easy,' Duggan said.

'What's on your mind, Matt?'

'I ain't forgot yuh, yuh dirty sonofabitch. Long as the other boys was around I couldn't take no chances. I had to bait my trap with

192

some nice cheese like that note.'

'When did you learn how to write?'

Duggan chuckled. 'The Williams filly taught me.'

Duggan placed his pistol on the lazy-board of one of the wagons. He spat on his hands. 'I'm agoin' to take the starch outa yuh, Shay.'

Sabin shifted. The man never had been normal. 'You're loco, Duggan. Those hills are crawling with Sioux.'

'They don't fight at night.'

'They hear a racket and they'll be around.'

'Racket? Hawww! I'll smash yuh, Shay.'

Sabin sighed. 'Come on then.'

He came on with short, plunging strides, pumping both thick arms like pistons. They smashed Sabin's guard aside. He went back, trying to block with forearms and elbows. He hit the ground from a right that struck like a pipe-axe. He got the boot twice before he made it to his feet.

Duggan wheezed laughter as they circled. Then he came on again. Sabin locked the thick arms under his elbows and brought up his knee into Duggin's groin. He broke free as Duggan grunted in pain, then lanced a left to Duggan's meaty jaw as the man doubled over. He chopped both hands at the base of the shaggy neck. Duggan crouched and ran awkwardly away.

Sabin took his own turn laughing. 'Come on back, kingpin!' he jeered.

Duggan snatched up something from the grass. It was a rusted pitchfork with the center tine broken off short. His lips drew back from his yellow teeth. He held the shaft in his right hand, halfway down, as he advanced in a crouch.

Sabin glanced at the pistol lying on the lazy-board. He darted for it but Duggan drove in hard with the fork. The tines hit the wagon. Sabin snatched back his arm an instant before they struck.

Sabin backed off, wetting his lips. If he ran he'd get it in the back like a harpoon. Duggan lunged. A tine scraped through Sabin's shirt, raking his left side. He gripped the shaft but Duggan backhanded him, driving him down on one knee. Sabin rolled over just as the fork plunged into the soft earth where he had been downed. Something rolled under him. He snatched up a four-foot length of heavy chain as he got to his feet.

Duggan charged. Sabin whirled the chain. The end smashed against Duggan's face. He gasped as he staggered sideways. Sabin swung again, catching Duggan across the chest. Duggan retreated, glancing at his pistol. He tried for it but Sabin moved like a cat. He got between the big man and the wagon. Duggan was hurt. His breath came harshly in his throat. He gripped his fork and held it like a musket at port arms, waiting for Sabin's attack.

Sabin darted on one side. Duggan thrust. Sabin reversed, backlashing with the chain. It whipped about Duggan's skull, the tip flicking into his left eye. Blood splattered from his face. He yelled hoarsely as he clapped his left hand against the smashed eye.

Sabin moved in, chopping with the doubled chain, raining blows on head and shoulders until Duggan went squirming back against the wagon. Duggan dropped the fork and ran in panic. Then he tripped over a broken wheel and went down.

Sabin threw the bloody chain away. Duggan groaned as he pawed at his eye. Then he began to fumble in his shirt. He was up on his feet with the knife in his hand before Sabin could grab the chain. Duggan's bloody face was like a mask straight from the steaming slums of hell. Then Sabin saw the knife clearly in the moonlight. He could not mistake it. It was the silver-chased knife which had been stolen from Miles' effects as he lay in the hospital.

There was no pity and no fear in Sabin now. He retreated before the half-blinded giant. Then he stooped and snatched up the pitchfork. Duggan seemed to be in a daze, but he did see the poised fork. For a second he stood there, and then he whirled, throwing the knife into the brush. He ran.

Sabin cast the heavy fork. One of the tines struck deeply beneath the left shoulderblade.

Duggan hurtled on, carried by the force of the blow and his own momentum. He went down, dead before he hit the ground. The fork shaft swayed a little as the big body twitched.

Sabin wiped the greasy cold sweat from his face. He hawked and spat to get rid of the sour taste in the back of his throat. He found his Colt and the knife. Then he dragged the heavy body to the waterside and rolled it in.

Sabin padded through the brush. He stopped. That tree over there had a shadow that was far too fat for it. Sabin cocked the Colt. Then he heard the faint sound of breathing.

'Come on out,' he said.

The man stepped out into the moonlight. It was Stacy Bascomb. The whole plot was etched on his face. He had stationed himself there to watch Duggan commit mayhem and murder on a man he couldn't fight himself.

'What's wrong with you?' Stacy asked shakily.

Sabin slid the Colt beneath his belt. 'Your champion failed,' he said softly. 'The show was spoiled, wasn't it?'

Stacy looked beyond the set-faced man in front of him. 'I'll call out to the guards,' he said. 'I saw you kill him.'

Sabin's left hand caught the trembling Stacy full across the mouth. His right drove Stacy to his knees. Then Sabin had him by the shirt front with his left hand bunched into the fine material. His right cut the handsome face into bloody ruin. Stacy sagged down on his knees, gripping Stacy about the thighs. 'For God's sake! Stop! Stop!'

Sabin dragged him to his feet. He whirled him about and planted a boot against his rump. Stacy Bascomb groveled on his hands and knees. Again and again Sabin booted him until the bloody-faced wretch scuttled through the woods to the shelter of the fort.

Sabin went to his tent. His mates were asleep. He stripped to the waist and examined the gash across his left ribs. It had been too damned close. One day he'd grip Stacy's scrawny neck until he gasped like a dying chicken. Sabin walked outside and let the fresh night wind dry the sweat on his body. But the wind could not blow away the foulness of Fort Bowen.

CHAPTER TWENTY-TWO

The hand gripped Sabin's shoulder. He opened his eyes and came up off his blankets, fighting hard.

'Hold it, Shay!' the voice roared.

The mists cleared. Sabin saw the angry face of Corporal Kinzie. 'Sorry,' he said.

Kinzie shook his head. 'Get dressed,' he

said. 'There's hell to pay. Khuyper wants to see you.'

'Uh—oh. Why?'

'Matt Duggan was found on a sand bank in the river with a pitchfork sticking in his back. Someone said you were seen near there last night.'

Cobb Howell, Warner Giddings and Blalock Lott stirred uneasily. 'That's what you was afraid of, cap'n,' Cobb said. 'So help me none of us done it, though.'

'I know,' Sabin said, and winked. 'Just keep your mouths shut and wait.'

Khuyper was in his quarters with Colonel Bascomb. Stacy stood against the back wall. His face was swollen almost beyond recognition.

Khuyper did not return Sabin's salute.

'Teamster Duggan was found dead this morning,' he said. 'You were seen near the emigrant wagons shortly after midnight, and then seen again coming from the woods beyond the wagons. What have you to say?'

Sabin looked past him at the battered Stacy. 'Nothing, sir.'

'You deny being there?'

'No, sir.'

Colonel Bascomb puffed at his cigar. 'I would like to prefer charges against him, suh.'

'Military or otherwise?' Sabin asked.

'Damn you!' Khuyper snarled. 'Keep a

civil tongue!'

Stacy pointed at Sabin. 'I saw him, I tell you,' he said thickly. 'It was him all right.'

'Go to hell,' Sabin said.

Khuyper stood up. 'I formally charge you with the murder of Teamster Matt Duggan. I hereby warn you that anything you say hereafter may be used against you.'

'You'll need witnesses,' Sabin said.

'You admit you did it then?' Stacy said eagerly.

'Stacy, you scaly bastard, I wouldn't even admit I was *here* to you.'

Colonel Bascomb said, 'If you were a gentleman, suh, my son would ask you out.'

Sabin laughed. 'Him? He hasn't got the guts of a louse. At least a louse will bite.'

Stacy's hands clawed empty air. He said, 'You—' in a strangled voice, and couldn't finish.

Khuyper looked at Corporal Kinzie. 'Place this man Shay in the guardhouse. Bucked and gagged as before. That will keep his tongue—'

The door opened, interrupting him. Katherine Williams walked in. Khuyper eyed her suspiciously. Stacy seemed to be looking right through her worn dress.

'I understand Trooper Sabin Shay is being charged with murder,' she said. 'It isn't true.'

Khuyper actually went pale. 'Get out of here,' he said.

She lowered her head. 'You have to hear me out,' she said, almost whispering. 'I know he could not have killed Matt Duggan.'

'Can you prove it?' Colonel Bascomb sneered.

'Yes. I know where he was from the time he came off guard until after one o'clock this morning.'

'Huh?' Khuyper recovered quickly. 'Where was he?'

She moistened her lips. A deep flush spread from her throat up to her hairline.

'Well?' Khuyper snapped.

'He—was with me. In one of the emigrant wagons.'

Stacy swallowed hard. Colonel Bascomb worked his cigar from one side of his mouth to the other. Khuyper just stared.

'She's lying,' Sabin said.

She shook her head. '*He's* lying to protect my reputation. He was with me.'

The three men glanced at each other. Khuyper sucked in his breath.

'Get out of here!' he said hoarsely. 'Get out of my sight—both of you!'

Outside, Sabin caught Katherine by the arms and shook her gently. 'You know what you've done to your reputation?' he said.

'Yes.'

'Thanks. I was in a bad spot in there.'

'You seem always to be in bad spots. I know they hate you.'

'You've made a choice bit of juicy gossip.'

She looked toward the distant hills. 'This is such a clean country,' she said softly. 'Too bad the people living out here cannot see how close they are to God.'

They walked toward the wagons. Women nodded to Katherine. They respected her now for her work among the sick. In a short time they would treat her like dirt.

'It was a courageous thing to do,' Sabin said.

She glanced sideways at him. 'You did kill him, didn't you?'

'Yes.'

'Why?'

'He meant to kill or maim me. This is a clean country, as you say, but it's a tough country too. Kill or be killed. The strong survive. The weak turn back or die.'

'My father once said that the cowards turn back and the weaklings die.'

'It's so.'

'I was a fool to come on, Sabin Shay.'

'Maybe it was meant to be. I'm a fatalist, Katherine.'

He left her at the wagons. He found Cobb Howell sitting on his blankets eating from his meat can.

'Yuh heard the news?' Howell queried.

'*I'm* the news, Cobb.'

'Yeh. I know the girl saved yer skin. But what I meant was, the telegraph line is through.'

'So?'

'A patrol from the east repaired the line. Sent a message the hostiles are swarmin' like buffalo gnats east of here, headin' for the fort. Half a thousand of 'em. Real shoppin' war party. Pony tails tied up and warpaint on their rumps. Led by a sure-'nough fighter too. Standin' Bear.'

It had to come, Sabin thought.

'Salt, pepper and gravel in the grease,' he said.

'Amen.'

'We can hold them off here.'

'Mebbe.' Howell spat. 'A rumor down to the sanitary sinks is thet Khuyper has been talked into escortin' Bascomb west outa the danger area.'

'Bascomb? How about the emigrants?'

Howell scraped his fork in the bottom of his meat can. 'Damn lousy fixin's they feed yuh here,' he growled.

'Yuh know how Khuyper feels. I hear from the cooks he's figgerin' on takin' enough calvary to protect Bascomb. Bascomb's animiles kin haul them fine waggins of his twict as fast as the emmygrants kin go.'

Sabin nodded. It was like Khuyper and Bascomb. Khuyper was a small edition of God at Fort Bowen.

CHAPTER TWENTY-THREE

Once Frank Khuyper made up his mind, with pressure from Clay Bascomb, he got into action at once. He chose the best horses and the best shots amongst the men for his escort company. Fifty men were to go along with Lieutenants Teale, Carlson and Burgeen, the best officers in his command.

Command of Fort Bowen fell to bumbling Captain Seb Horton. He was an expert in Army paperwork but in nothing else.

Angry talk bubbled and boiled in the emigrant camp. Khuyper refused to take them along. Sam Nelson tried to have a message sent to Fort Laramie conerning the matter, but the line had gone dead again. Fort Bowen had but half a hundred men fit for duty and most of them were infantry. Khuyper lined up his command at dusk. Sabin saw Marianne Bascomb helped into her sumptuous Dearborn. The story was that she was ill, but Sabin knew she was halfseas over with vermouth and fear. Sabin started as he saw a slim woman come from the emigrant camp carrying a carpetbag. It was Katherine Williams.

Sabin stopped her. 'You're not going with them?'

'Yes. I'm going, Sabin.'

'But why?' he asked desperately.

'There is no work for me here. Colonel Bascomb offered to double my wages if I went along to help Marianne. She's ill.'

'Drunk,' he said.

'Judge not, lest ye be judged, Sabin Shay.'

'For God's sake, woman! Your chances of surviving out there are no better than they are here. Possibly worse.'

'My reputation *has* suffered here. I want to go on to Oregon.'

'I thought you hated their souls.'

'I did once. It doesn't matter now.'

'Is there no way I can make you see the light?'

Her clear eyes held his. 'There may be.'

'What is it?'

She looked away. 'You must know that yourself.'

Sabin shoved back his forage cap. 'You've got me licked,' he said.

'Shay!' roared a sergeant. 'Shay! Dammit! Where are you?'

Sabin turned. 'Good-bye Katherine,' he said quietly.

She nodded and walked toward the Dearborn. A teamster handed her up into the coach. She slammed the door shut and let down the canvas blind.

Sabin stood there watching the train pull out. The shadowy wagons and troopers disappeared into the purple darkness. In time there was nothing left to mark their passing but a smell of bitter dust in the night air.

★   ★   ★

Sam Nelson had called a council of his men. They demanded an escort from bumbling Seb Horton. Horton was flustered. This went beyond precise paperwork. It called for the judgment of a uniformed Solomon and Horton was far from being that. He flatly refused the use of any troops, claiming, quite rightly, that he could not afford to lose any men at all.

Horton did send out scouts at dawn. They returned at noon with a report that the immediate hills were empty of hostiles, but that they had seen much dust to the west, in a great valley beyond the hills. Khuyper had served one good purpose in some minds; he had drawn the hostiles after him.

Nelson saw his chance. He marshaled his wagons in the late afternoon. Half a dozen of the worst ones had been stripped to furnish parts and ironwork for better vehicles. Their poorest horses and mules were slaughtered for extra meat. Horton grudgingly allowed Nelson the use of an extra supply of trade rifles which had been stored in the little post and overlooked by the raiders.

Sabin spoke with Nelson before he left. 'You're sticking your neck out, Sam.'

Nelson shifted his chew. 'I'm leadin' these people to Oregon. Sojers or no sojers. Might be that Khuyper has led the hostiles off.'

'There's enough of them to go around,' Sabin said.

'Hellfire. I fit Injuns afore yuh was outa diapers!'

'You'll lose your hair, Sam.'

Nelson snorted. 'I ain't kissin' Horton's fat rump for no favors. We got extry rifles now. Most of the wimmen kin load and shoot. I'll get through!' He stamped off.

The emigrants pulled out at dusk, as Khuyper had. A line of emigrant outriders surrounded the wagons, but it was pitifully thin. Many of them were boys. They rode as if they had learned to ride on plowhorses. If the hostiles, the finest light cavalry in the world, swept down on them, they wouldn't have a chance.

Sabin found Cobb Howell, Charlie Kester and George Fletcher in his tent when he returned.

'Meeting,' Kester said. 'Kinston Forbes is on guard duty.'

Sabin dropped on his blankets and accepted a cigar from Fletcher.

'This is our chance,' Kester said. 'We can pull out of here before Horton knows a thing. The hostiles will be after those wagons like trout after grasshoppers. What do you say, Cap'n Shay?'

'I'm thinking of those women and kids out there,' Sabin said.

'Yankee squaws and Yankee kids,' Fletcher said.

'Americans,' Sabin said.

'Listen to him!' Fletcher jeered.

'Shut up!' Kester said.

Sabin chewed at the dry cigar. 'Supposing I talk Horton into letting us go after the emigrants? He has no damned use for Galvanized Yankees.'

'Fat chance,' Cobb Howell said.

'If we make a break we lose men. We haven't enough as it is to break through the Sioux. I can grease the way if I can talk him into ordering us out.'

Fletcher rubbed his jaw. 'He's stupid, but he ain't *that* stupid.'

'You're an expert on stupidity,' Kester said dryly. 'Go ahead, Cap'n Shay. You've been using your *cabeza* while we've been milling around.'

Sabin went into headquarters. Horton was presiding behind Khuyper's old desk. He drummed on it with fat fingers. 'What's your angle, Shay?' he asked suspiciously.

'Khuyper may be cut off. That's *his* responsibility. But those emigrants were *your* responsibility. If Nelson gets wiped out, the department commander will place the blame squarely on your shoulders, sir.'

Horton was badly shaken. Sweat dewed his

fat face. 'I'm up for promotion,' he said as though to himself.

Sabin timed his next words. He knew Horton secretly feared the lean Texans, and there were too many of them left at the little post to give him much peace of mind. 'The Galvanized Yankees are trained Indian fighters, sir. You could send us to help Nelson.'

Horton reacted as if Sabin had read his mind. 'Do you take me for a fool?' he shouted. 'Get out of here!'

Sabin saluted and walked outside. Seb Horton paced back and forth. He had never trusted those hard-eyed Texas bastards. Shay had been right when he had said Nelson was the post commander's responsibility, and that placed the blame for any misfortune squarely on the shoulders of Sebastian Horton.

Sabin paused fifty yards away from headquarters in sight of the front door. He didn't have long to wait. Horton's plump figure showed in the doorway.

'Shay!' he yelled. 'Round up Mister Degnan and Mister Kretch along with Sergeant Schmidt! Get them here on the double!'

*   *   *

Sebastian Horton had clutched at a straw. Once Sabin's idea had made itself secure in his mind, he had adopted it as his own. First Lieutenant James Degnan, an infantryman whose chief claim to military fame was the fact he had been the best poker player at Fort Laramie, was to be in charge of the 'flying relief column' as Horton fatuously termed the little force. Second Lieutenant August Kretch was in charge of the cavalry. He had never heard a shot fired in anger within half a mile of himself.

Horton assigned two escort wagons to carry the dozen infantrymen he had allowed Degnan. There wasn't any doubt in the Texans' minds as to why he was sending them along. It was Sergeant Manfred Schmidt who worried Sabin the most. His pale blue eyes kept Sabin and his grinning Texans under constant inspection. Sabin knew damned well that Schmidt would fight them alone if he had to, to keep them under the colors of his adopted country.

Hamish Hume leaned against the corral wall to watch Sabin place his cantle and pommel packs on his bay. 'So you're on your way West?' he asked quietly.

Sabin nodded.

'There is something going on here I do not like,' Hamish Hume said. 'There is a lot of land out there.'

'I've been there, Hamish.'

'I'd like to go along.'

'Saddle a horse.'

'It isn't as easy as all that. There's plenty of responsibility for me here. Thank God I sent ten men back on duty in the last two days.'

'The post is safe enough. The hostiles won't buck up against walk-a-heaps firing rifles from a rest, and behind stout walls. They respect that type of defence.'

'But how about you? Those officers are a poor lot.'

Sabin leaned back against his saddle. 'My men can take care of themselves out there.'

'This is good-bye then.'

'I'm not dead yet.'

'No,' Hamish Hume said. 'But dead or alive, I am not sure I will see you again.'

Sabin grinned. 'We'll see each other again, Hamish. It's in the cards.'

'Perhaps.' Hume gripped Sabin's shoulder. 'You must act before you think. I wish it were otherwise. You're a young man, Sabin. A man with great capabilities and a fine future, *if* you can find yourself. Good-bye, my friend.' The surgeon walked off into the shadows.

A lonely feeling crept over Sabin as he led his bay to where the detail was lining up.

Horton bustled out of his office. 'Now, Degnan and Kretch, you must be wary. Use discretion. Remember those emigrants are depending on you.'

Kretch looked as though King Arthur had just invited him to sit at the Round Table.

Degnan swung up on his horse.

'Mount! Fours Right! Walk Ho!'

They filed down the fort road and turned left on the river road. In a few moments they were out of sight. Horton turned to his officers. 'Corral all stock. Double the guards. Shutter the windows. Place combustibles in all outbuildings ready to fire them in case of attack.'

Lieutenant Cope saluted. Lieutenant Rogers grinned. 'How about a little game tonight, boys? he asked.

Horton drew himself up to his full five feet seven inches. 'Sir!' he barked. 'I am in full charge of a military post of the United States Government! There will be no laxity in discipline here! No frivolity! To your posts!' He bustled into his office.

'My God,' Rogers said.

Cope smiled at him. 'Funny thing, Norton. The fat little bastard *means* it too. God help us all.'

CHAPTER TWENTY-FOUR

The sun was just tipping the hills when Sabin and Cobb Howell returned to the little column. 'Sir,' Sabin said to Lieutenant Degnan, 'there are hostiles betwen the Bascomb train and the emigrant train. They

211

seem more interested in the Bascomb train.'

Degnan bit his lip. 'They're after Khuyper then.'

'I think so, sir.'

'How many of them?'

'It's hard to say, Mister Degnan. We saw about fifty, but there must be many more of them in hiding.'

Degnan was more worried about getting caught than he was of helping the emigrants. 'Damn Khuyper!' he snapped. 'With our combined commands, and both trains together, we might have had a better chance.'

'It's too late now,' Sabin said.

Degnan nodded. 'We'll rest here. No fires. We'll go on in three hours.'

But it was closer to noon when they moved on through cut-up land, crossed by shallow streams and broken by low hill masses. The men were nervous, constantly shifting in their saddles to scan the brooding hills. At dusk they reached a low, flat-topped hill. They bivouacked off the skyline and again ate cold rations. Sabin, Howell and Kinston Forbes went out on a scout. They could see no lights in the great valley but the emigrants couldn't be far ahead. Nelson must have been pushing them to overtake Bascomb's outfit.

Forbes shifted his chew and spat. 'This is our chance,' he said quietly.

Sabin turned. 'The wagons aren't safe yet.'

'To hell with 'em.'

'Damn you, Forbes. You haven't got the sense God gave a louse!'

'Watch what yuh say, Shay.'

Howell kneed his bay in between them. 'Cut it,' he said.

Forbes thrust out his chin. 'He's been agin us ever since he got tied up with that Williams filly. We're out far enough now to make our break.'

'We wait!' Sabin snapped.

Forbes spurred his horse close to Sabin. His heavy carbine rose and fell. Sabin slid from the saddle and lay still.

'Kinston!' Howell roared. 'What for did yuh do thet?'

'Listen,' Forbes said coldly. 'We're pullin' out. You go back and get the boys. Yuh can work it out.'

'What about Cap'n Shay?'

Forbes grinned. 'He's goin' with us. Conscious or unconscious. Now git the boys. We can be miles on the way by dawn. Jump up some dust, amigo. *Vamonos!*'

★　　★　　★

There was a faint suggestion of the false dawn in the sky when Cobb Howell and the Galvanized Yankees jingled up through the darkness. They brought a prisoner with them, lashed and gagged atop a rangy bay. Sabin squinted, trying to identify the captive.

213

His head ached as though he had been on a tequila bust.

'For God's sake!' Forbes yelled. 'What for did yuh bring Schmidt along?'

Howell slid from his saddle and eased his crotch. 'It was either bring him or kill him.'

Charlie Kester walked over to Sabin. 'It was easy. There was only three beetle-crushers on guard. Cobb Indians up on them, buffaloes them, and then gets the boys together. Degnan and Kretch was asleep. Only Schmidt gets wise. We had to take him along.'

Sabin fingered the knot on his head. 'Well, you've got everything the way you all wanted it.'

'Yuh sound riled,' Jesse Tinsley said.

'I am. Those emigrants might need us.'

'They didn't even know we was out here,' Fletcher said.

They know the hostiles are,' Sabin said quietly.

'Let's move out,' Kester said.

'Where to?' Jerry LaValle asked.

Without bothering to answer, Kester took Sabin's weapons from Forbes and handed them to Sabin. 'Lead out, sir.'

Sabin holstered his Colt and gripped his carbine. 'I'll go along. I haven't any choice. But you bastards can do your own commanding. I'm no longer your officer.'

Kester said, 'This is what you wanted,

214

back at Fort MacNaughton, Cap'n Shay. We're free now. We've got plenty grub and good horses. We pinched three mules and loaded them with supplies.'

'I *said* he was riled,' Tinsley said.

Sabin swung up on his horse and kneed it close to Schmidt. He took the gag from the non-com's mouth. 'Gott verdamnt!' Schmidt roared.

Sabin cut loose the sergeant's wrist bonds. '*Vamonos*,' he said.

Schmidt rubbed his wrists. 'No. I go along. I gedt my chance. I arrest you all yedt.'

'Go to hell, you Dutch bastard,' Fletcher said.

'Cherman I am! I go along!'

Forbes raised his carbine. 'Git!'

Sabin drew his Colt and twirled the cylinder. 'The first man who harms him gets it in the belly,' he said coldly.

Howell shrugged. 'Let's pull foot. Let him go.'

They rode west, passing the non-com. But Schmidt was a man with a one-track mind. He rode on a hundred yards behind the pack mules, unarmed and alone, but determined that he'd bring those men back to the fold. In his book they were United States Cavalrymen, and by God, Manfred Schmidt was going to bring them back if he had to dog them clear to Oregon.

CHAPTER TWENTY-FIVE

The heat covered the deep draw with a hot blanket. The horses stood with bowed heads near the water hole. The men dozed on the ground with forage caps tilted over their eyes.

Sabin lay at the lip of the draw, studying a movement across the valley through the fieldglasses Howell had stolen from Degnan. 'It's them all right, Cobb,' he said over his shoulder. 'Dog Soldiers. Crazy Dogs. Stronghearts. Massing behind that hill. I swear I saw Standing Bear talking big out in front of them.'

Kester took the glasses. 'The emigrants are still at the crick. You think the hostiles are after them?'

'Uh-uh. Not now. Nelson is in his defensive circle.'

'Where in hell is Khuyper?'

'On the far side of that rocky hill, I'd say.'

'The hostiles are after him then?'

'Keno.'

'What do we do?' Howell asked.

'Sit tight,' Sabin said.

Manfred Schmidt sat on a rock beyond the waterhole. Howell grinned. 'Bullhead, ain't he?'

'You have to admire him,' Sabin said.

Kester wiped his sweaty face. 'You want to

take a closer look at the war party?'

'Might as well. I sure as hell can't sleep with all this going on.'

They rode west, keeping behind the line of hills. A half a mile from the hill they saw the Bascomb train. The wagons had been formed into an irregular square. The sun glinted on metal. A line of cavalrymen had formed in front of the wagons. A thin line of warriors faced them from the west. Sabin could see a mass of warriors formed in a draw to the north, unseen by the troopers because of a slanting ridge.

'That Khuyper,' Kester said. 'What's he planning to do?'

Sabin wet cracked lips. 'He's going to charge them. The fool!'

The troopers moved out at a walk, stepped up to a trot, and then suddenly broke into a fast run. The wind tore the brazen notes of the Charge into ragged shreds. The thin line of hostiles parted. They fired from the far side of their ponies. The troopers drew up, reformed, then charged back toward the wagons. The hostiles scattered again, winding the big cavalry horses.

The thin line drew off to one side and waited. Khuyper led his sweating men on again. They went up the rise, hell-for-leather, pistols at the ready and sabers flashing in the sun. Up, up and over the rise after the retreating bucks. Then the main body of

217

hostiles moved, slowly at first, and then with a massed charge that struck the troopers like a load of buckshot at close range. Dust veiled the clash. Pistols popped like grease in a gigantic skillet. Then Sioux, Cheyenne and Arapahoe rifles roared.

The troopers shredded down the bloody slope, riding wildly, looking back over their shoulders with white faces. A third of them were gone. Warriors cut in to snap up stragglers. Then a thin sickle of racing brown horsemen shot in between the retreating troopers and the wagons. The scattered troopers pelted over a rise to the east of the wagons and looked back to see a great wheel of warriors between them and the wagons, beginning the slow circling attack which would tighten and tighten until the Cossacks of the Plains would be firing at pointblank range into the wagons.

Sabin groaned. Khuyper had done the one thing he should never have done. He had allowed his force to be bloodied and then cut off from the wagons. Sabin stood up.

'What the hell's the matter with you?' Kester said. 'Get down!'

Sabin gripped the reins of his bay. 'Go on back,' he said.

'Where yuh think you're goin'?' Howell asked.

Sabin jerked a thumb toward the surrounded wagons. Rifle flames dotted the thick dust. Sabin swung up and spurred the bay down into the draw which led toward the fight.

'A strange man,' Cobb said as he shifted his chew. 'I don't hardly know him no more.'

Kester snorted. 'You dumb bastard. Don't you know what's the matter with him?'

'Can't say as I do right now.'

'It's that girl.'

'Sure. Sure. I know thet. But he ain't about to give her much help going down there alone.'

Kester rubbed his jaw and looked back toward the district draw where the Galvanized Yankees waited for darkness. 'Yeh,' he said quietly. 'Let's get back to the boys. I got some talking to do.'

★   ★   ★

Sabin picketed the bay in a draw. He bellied up and hid out in a clump of brush. Some of the hostiles weren't more than two hundred yards from him. They had drawn off from the wagons for a breather. Reeking scalps hung from bloody lances. They had scattered the Mila Hanska with little loss to themselves. The people in the wagons were soft for the killing.

Sabin studied the terrain with his glasses. Here and there he spotted the lone body of a scalped trooper. Sabin estimated Khuyper's losses at about fifty percent. The rest of his demoralized men were scattered through the broken country to the south. Sabin lowered his glasses and rested his head on his forearms. He had never felt so alone in his whole life. There was no chance to break into the circle of warriors and get her out of the wagons. He had thought of starting a fire in the grass, but it wasn't dry enough to sustain a real covering fire. That left one alternative. Get close to the wagons, look for Katherine, and kill her before those hot greasy hands touched her body.

The warriors began a slow rifle fire against the wagon defenders. They wriggled through the grass and rocks, firing and then moving on to a new position. Sabin raised his glasses again. The fine German lens picked out the broad face of Standing Bear. The chief was squatting with a group of veteran warriors. Sabin fingered his Sharps. The range wasn't impossible, but killing Standing Bear would not stop the attack, and it sure as hell would stop Sabin Shay.

Minutes ticked past. A steady leaden rain of fire thudded against the Bascomb wagons. There were about twenty-five men in the smoky square—and two women.

Sabin sensed, rather than saw, the movement behind him. He turned slowly, raising himself up on one elbow. They were all there, sitting their sweating horses. Every living Texan from Sabin's old company, looking up at him with expressionless faces. Charlie Kester kneed his horse toward the bottom of the slope. 'You said you weren't our officer, no more, Cap'n Shay, but you can't get rid of us as easy as all that.'

Sabin slid down the slope. 'Get these men out of here! The draws and ridges are crawling with Sioux and Cheyennes!'

Cobb Howell grunted. 'My maw allus said I'd come to no good end. Helpin' Yankees! Jeeesus!'

Tim Casey shoved back his forage cap. 'We was figerin' on goin' west.'

'We are,' Kester said. 'Right through a passel of Sioux.'

Warner Giddings grinned at Sabin. He tapped his shining trumpet. 'I ain't had much chance to use this horn.'

'Makes a man sick,' Forbes snapped. 'Here we got a chance to cut stick and we got to fool around the business end of a war party.'

'Sit here on yore butt then,' Giddings said.

Jesse Tinsley shifted his chew and spat juicily. 'I got an eye on one of them Puke fillies back there in Nelson's waggins. 'Pears to me, if'n these hostiles take Bascomb's waggins, there ain't goin' to be anything to stop them from takin' Nelson's waggins but we 'uns.'

Sabin glowered balefully at them. 'Get out of here,' he said. 'We haven't got a chance against these red bastards.'

'Listen to him,' Cobb Howell said.

'Lost his guts,' Gus Feichter said.

Jesse Tinsley rode forward and handed Sabin a lance. 'Picked this up on the trail,' he said. 'Might make a good guidon staff if'n a man *had* a guidon.'

Sabin stared at the expressionless dusty faces. 'You damned romantic fools,' he said. He reached inside his shirt and took out the stained and torn guidon of Shay's Independent Frontier Company. He fastened it to the Indian lance. The wind snapped it out.

'Never thought I'd see thet again,' Todd Shafter said.

'I'd admire to carry it, suh,' Chase Corby said.

Sabin handed him the guidon.

'I aim to get those women out of that wagon ring,' he said. 'Anyone who wants to leave can do so.'

No one moved. *'Bueno!'* Sabin said.

'This is all very well,' Kinston Forbes drawled, 'but I ain't about to go chargin' out there whistlin' The Yellow Rose Of Texas whilst them hostiles pepper hell outa me. They's too many of 'em, Cap'n Shay, and yuh damn well know it—*suh!'*

The steady sound of the rifle fire came to them fitfully as the vagrant wind shifted. Sabin wiped the sweat from his face. 'If we wait much longer, Kinston,' he said, 'there won't be any reason for us to go out there at all.' They looked at each other and then away, each man trying to hide the sudden fear in his eyes.

Sabin jerked his head. 'Cobb Howell! Take a *pasear* to the west, keeping well to the north. See how far back the hostiles are.'

Cobb saluted and spurred his horse up the draw. Sabin nodded at Kester. 'Keep the company here. If the hostiles come this way, drop back under cover, but don't put up a fight unless there's no chance of breaking away.'

'Yes, sir.'

'I'm scouting south. Somewhere around here there's a place where we can break through.'

Sabin led his horse south along the draw. Now and then he bellied up to the top of the draw. They were still softening the defense of the wagon ring. Now and then a wisp of smoke would snake through the grass and hover until the distant sound of the shot caught up with it. A white man lay in front of the wagons clutching a rifle. Sabin knew he was dead.

A mile from the waiting company he came upon a dun horse grazing in the draw. The dun's saddle had slid to one side and blood showed on its flank. Beyond the horse a trooper lay on his back, both bloody hands

223

gripping an arrow shaft which protruded from his right side. His mouth and eyes were open. Flies buzzed lazily about them and his reddened hands.

Sabin ground-reined the bay and padded up the draw. He began to belly up the slope. Then he felt, rather than heard, the movement behind him. He turned, sweeping back the hammer of his Sharps. It was too late. Frank Khuyper stood there with a cocked Colt in his hand, the muzzle centered on Sabin's belly. Sabin lowered the Sharps very slowly. Khuyper looked wild. Six troopers, dusty and sweaty and fear-ridden, were huddling in the bottom of the draw. Sabin stood up and raised his hands.

'Where's your commanding officer?' Khuyper snapped.

Sabin wet his lips. The hand holding that pistol was shaking from suppressed rage. 'I have none, sir,' he lied.

'Deserted again, eh?'

Sabin glanced at the men. Khuyper had led them into a trap from which only fantastic luck had saved them. Some of them were looking up the draw, telegraphing their wish to get the hell out of there in a hurry and to hell with the hindmost.

'I was separated from Mr. Degnan's command,' Sabin said.

'You're alone then?' Khuyper asked craftily.

224

'Yes.'

'You lie, you Rebel bastard!' Khuyper said. He thrust out his free hand. 'There's a unit up this draw. Who's in command?'

'I don't know, sir.'

Khuyper raised his head. 'Then we'll damned well find out, won't we?'

Sabin shrugged. He walked to his horse and gripped the reins. Khuyper walked up behind him. 'Take us to them,' he said. 'Under cover. You understand.' He shoved the pistol muzzle against Sabin's back.

They slogged up the draw. Yellow dust wreathed up about them. Sabin glanced back. He could have sworn there was one less trooper behind the officer.

Half a mile from the waiting Galvanized Yankees, Khuyper came to a halt. 'Corporal Kostby!' he called.

The non-com came forward.

'Keep the men here. Shay! Up that rise!'

Sabin walked up the rise, hearing Khuyper puffing behind him. At the top of the rise they dropped. They could see one of Sabin's men on guard. The rest of them were in the draw. Wind had wrapped the guidon about the lance pole.

Khuyper nodded. 'There's enough,' he said to himself.

'Sir?'

'Enough, combining my men and those men there, to take the Sioux in the flank.'

Sabin glanced down into the draw. Not one of the troopers was left. Nothing was left but a wraith of yellow dust to mark their passage.

Khuyper talked on. 'I hurt them with that charge. I bled them. One more and I'll have them.'

Sabin eyed him. There was something radically wrong with the man. Sabin eased down the slope a little. Khuyper moved swiftly. There was nothing wrong with his reflexes. The Colt leveled on Sabin's head. 'Don't move, damn you! You're going along. We're all going down there again.'

'You'll never come back,' Sabin said.

'*I'll* get back.'

Sabin tried to shift so as to reach his Colt but Khuyper's eyes drilled into his. Then the officer stood up. 'What guidon is that?' he asked.

The stained guidon had unwrapped itself from the lance pole. Sabin got up on his knees. 'Take a good look, Khuyper,' he said quietly.

'It isn't—isn't a regulation Army guidon.'

Sabin planted his left foot on the ground and tensed himself.

Khuyper paled beneath the dust on his face. 'I've seen it before.'

'You have.'

'Where?'

Sabin stood up. 'At the Badwater,' he said.

Khuyper stepped back a little. He glanced

226

uncertainly toward the guidon. 'Corporal Kostby!' he called out of the side of his mouth.

Sabin shifted a little.

'Corporal Kostby!' Khuyper yelled down the slope.

Sabin's left hooked home to Khuyper's jaw at the same time his right hand reached across to grip the gun wrist. Khuyper staggered back, but he held his grip on the Colt. He snapped a shot just as Sabin drove in, arms outheld, and missed. Sabin butted Khuyper back with a shoulder while he gripped the cursing officer about the waist.

They went down the slope sideways, rolling over and over in a welter of dust and loose stones. Khuyper lost his Colt. He clawed at Sabin's holstered sidearm. Sabin kneed him in the guts. They broke apart.

Khuyper wiped the blood from his mouth. He bent his shoulders a little and went into a slight crouch. His eyes narrowed as Sabin circled to his right. Then the officer charged. Sabin met the attack with a left that straightened Khuyper out. He felt the jolt of the blow and then crossed with a right which sprawled Khuyper sideways, staggering for balance. He didn't make it. Down he went, blood dripping from his nose and mouth to stain the yellow dust.

Sabin rubbed big hands on his thighs. 'Get up, sir,' he said. 'I'm not through yet.'

Khuyper groaned a little. He got on his hands and knees. Then he moved with surprising swiftness, ripping a double-barreled derringer from inside his shell jacket. It puffed flame and smoke, sending a slug inches above Sabin's head. Sabin jumped sideways, closed in, kicked the derringer away from the yelling officer, and then went down heavily as his foot turned on a stone.

Khuyper was on him like a cat. His strong fingers dug into Sabin's throat. Sabin hammered at Khuyper's ribs but the officer hung on like grim death. The sky whirled. Sabin saw nothing but the two icy blue eyes fixed with the fascination of death for Sabin Shay. Sabin got a knee up into Khuyper's crotch and drove it up in desperate strength. The grip weakened. Again and again Sabin kneed the cursing man until Khuyper released his hold and rolled away, clutching his groin. Sabin righted himself, laboring painfully to draw breath.

Khuyper pawed for the derringer in the dusty grass. Sabin staggered toward him and kicked savagely again and again until Khuyper was down, his chest rising and falling in his rage and fatigue. Sabin gripped him by the back of his sweat-soaked jacket and jerked hard. Khuyper lurched to his feet. He threw up his arms as Sabin smashed blow after blow at his face until once again he was on his back staring up into the face of the man he had sworn to kill.

'Get up,' Sabin said. 'You wanted to know what guidon that was. I'll tell you. That's the guidon of Shay's Independent Frontier Company.'

Khuyper heaved himself up on his feet. He closed with Sabin. His knee came up into Sabin's groin. He jerked Sabin's Colt from its holster and cocked it. Sabin smashed the Colt upward with his left forearm and sank a right deep into Khuyper's belly. The Colt roared inches from his head, half-blinding him. Then he tore the weapon away from Khuyper. He cast it aside. Khuyper turned to run. Sabin gripped his shoulder and spun him about. Then he really went to work. He cut the mouth and smashed the fine nose. Teeth broke beneath his battering fists. Khuyper turned to run again. Sabin reached down for the Colt but something held him from shooting.

Khuyper sprinted up the draw. Then the lone horseman blocked his way. A slim Cheyenne with a drawn bow. Khuyper screamed once. The shaft struck him in the forehead and jutted there, quivering as if it were alive and striving to burrow deeper. Sabin jumped for the horse he had left ground-reined fifty feet away, with his Sharps slung to the saddle.

The Cheyenne leaped his paint horse across the dead officer, nocking another broadhead arrow to his bowstring as he did so. Sabin snapped a shot from his Colt. The Cheyenne drew back the bowstring.

A shot cracked flatly from the lip of the draw. The Cheyenne slid from his racing mount and hit the ground fifty feet from Sabin. Sabin stopped and looked up. Manfred Schmidt sat his horse, with a smoking carbine in his big hands.

'Thanks,' Sabin said.

Schmidt slid his mount down the slope. He nodded at Khuyper. 'Deadt?'

'Yes.'

The blue eyes held Sabin's. 'I did nodt see anything else,' he said quietly.

Sabin flicked blood from his abraded hands. 'You know damned well who killed him, Schmidt.'

'Yes. Howell iss back. The poys are gedding restless.'

Sabin swung up on his horse and spurred it along the draw. Schmidt followed him.

CHAPTER TWENTY-SIX

Cobb Howell squatted in the shade of his lathered horse. He inspected Sabin curiously as he slid from his horse. 'Yuh been fightin' them hostiles alone?' he asked.

'I met an old friend of ours. Captain

Khuyper.'

Every man stood up and reached for carbine or pistol. Sabin shook his head. 'He's dead. Forget about him. We've got work to do.'

Howell stood up. 'They's two places I found,' he said. 'Look here.' He went down on one knee and traced a map in the dust with his forefinger. 'They's two ridges north of here. Runnin' east-west generally. South of the ridges is where the waggins is penned. The hostiles is massing in the valley between the ridges. Howsomever, at this end of the valley they're in, they's a place where brush grows thick over a low ridge that cuts acrost the valley. They's a place there yuh kin ride plumb into the valley where the waggins is and them hostiles cain't see yuh.'

'A score of men,' Kinston Forbes said.

'Ain't no use lookin' back for help,' Warner Giddings said.

Sabin frowned thoughtfully. 'You said there were *two* places, Cobb?'

'I did. West of the valley where the hostiles is, a man kin ride south without bein' seen. Could come in from the west down on them waggins easy enough. Might be two-three hunnerd yards from a hiding place. A long ride if'n yore bein' shot at, which is quite likely.'

Sabin wet his lips. He had but a handful of men to cast on the scales of chance. They

231

could be used just once, and that rightly, and it was up to him to choose the time and place. He had no one to lean back on; no one to consult.

The firing grew heavier over the lip of the draw. 'The wagons were getting it hot and heavy, sir,' Denny O'Brien called down.

'Any signs of the hostiles massing?'

'There's a lot of dust behind that north ridge.'

Sabin mulled it over. 'There's no use trying to make it sound as though we hold the bull by the horns,' he told his men.

'What do you want us to do?' Kester asked.

'Time's awastin',' Corby said.

Sabin looked at Warner Giddings. 'How's your wind?'

'Fine, suh.'

'Can you work behind the Sioux and come out west of the wagons where that low ridge is?'

'*Alone*, suh?'

Sabin nodded.

Giddings' Adam's apple bobbed in his thin throat. 'Yes, Cap'n Shay.'

'*Bueno*. Cut north of here. Then west. Come down behind that far ridge. Watch the hostiles. When you see them top their ridge to come down on those wagons I want you to show up on that ridge and blow hell out of that trumpet. Blow the Charge or any damned thing else. But keep blowing.'

'What—what do I do then, suh?'

Sabin smiled. 'That will be up to you. You'll see what I mean when the time comes. *Vamonos!*'

The minutes ticked past while little Warner Giddings rode north and then west through a country thick with Sioux.

*   *   *

Sabin guided his small command through the thick brush. Manfred Schmidt silently led his horse along behind the Texans. It was as Howell had said. They were in the same valley as the Sioux, for they could hear the noise of the warriors on the far side of the mass of rocks and brush which shielded them from the hostiles. Bitter dust drifted over them as hundreds of unshod hoofs churned it up.

'Wonder how the kid is?' Howell ventured.

'He's outa *this* anyways,' Forbes said.

Sabin and Kester worked their way up the ridge to observe the warriors. 'There's sure a slew of them,' Sabin said. 'Odds of ten to one, Charlie.'

'Usual Texican odds,' Kester boasted hollowly.

The warriors were forming on the slopes now. Sioux, Cheyenne and Arapahoe. They knew it would be a good day for them. The firing from the wagons had weakened. Wakan

233

Tanka was smiling on the Sioux. Maheo had brought good fortune to the Cheyenne. There would be Thunder Music in the Arapahoe camp. The feathered and painted horsemen lined up under their different sub-chiefs and veteran warriors of many coups. Sabin's eyes narrowed as he saw the thick-bodied chief ride along the line of braves. There was no mistaking Standing Bear. Sabin focused his glasses on the chief while Kester shaded the lens to prevent light reflection.

Standing Bear swam hazily into view. His warbonnet rippled in the wind. He was ready for war. Lance, rifle, bow and quiver, pipe-ax, revolving pistol and scalping knife. He halted his spotted gray and began to speak, exhorting his men. Sabin wanted to try a long shot but he knew better. The time had not come.

'They're getting ready. He's talking it up,' Kester said in a strained voice.

Sabin cased the glasses. 'Have the horses led up below the crest of the ridge. And for God's sake, Charlie, don't let any man be seen!'

The first sergeant slid down the ridge.

Sabin watched Standing Bear flourish his lance and ride up to the top of the ridge. There he drew rein and proudly sat his gray. The warriors massed on the ridge, a splendid, barbaric body of the finest light cavalry in the world.

Sabin went down to his horse and led him to the company rendezvous. Down in the valley the wagons stood in their defensive square. The tilts flapped in the strong wind. The wind ruffled the beard of the dead man who lay beyond the wagons.

'I hope he made it,' Sabin said, looking at the ridge to the west. There was no sign of life on it.

Standing Bear kneed his horse away from his warriors and started slowly down the ridge toward the wagons.

'Now,' Sabin said. 'Now, Giddings—*now*!'

The warriors were following their leader. Their left flank was no more than two hundred yards from the waiting Texans.

'For God's sake,' Kester husked. 'Where are you, Giddings?'

The answer came as the kid showed up on the ridge. The sun glinted from his polished trumpet as he flourished it and placed it to his lips. The warriors were at a trot now, bunching a little for the hell-for-leather charge which would take them clean through the wagon square. Then Giddings lipped into the brazen, thrilling notes of The Charge. The wind picked up the call and carried it across the valley.

Standing Bear turned his horse toward the ridge where the kid sat his bay. Behind the chief, the warriors were urging on their horses, presenting their broad flank to Sabin's men.

'Now,' Sabin said.

'Sabers?' Kester asked.

'Hell no. That's Yankee stuff. Pistols.'

'There's a hell of a lot of 'em down there,' someone said behind Sabin.

'Just pick a redskinned sonofabitch and charge,' Cobb Howell said.

Sabin did not look back. He drew his pistol and sank the steel into his bay. The big horse lifted easily into a run down the rough slope. A warrior saw them and screamed to his mates. But it was too late for a defense. These weren't the usual clumsy, slow-riding Mila Hanska, but a different breed of foemen.

Then the Texans roared into the soft unprotected flank, pistols snapping at ten and five feet, smashing flesh and bone with hot lead. Warriors and ponies went down in a bone-breaking tangle.

Sabin went through it in a wild haze of smoke and noise, dropping two warriors. The Texans struck the milling warriors like a flash flood, spilling the bucks down the slope like tenpins. The warriors milled on the slippery grass, some of them trying to get back up the ridge, others trying to get down into the valley. Some of them hammered on toward the wagons. A volley ripped into the hostiles from the wagons, driving them back. But it was a pitifully weak defense.

Three of Sabin's men had fallen in the

spume of smoke and dust. Sabin drew up and slid from his saddle. 'Prepare to fight on foot!' he roared above the din. 'Dismount! Horseholders in!'

The horses were led off as Standing Bear rallied some of his toughest warriors for a charge. The Texans lined the lip of a shallow hollow, thrusting their carbines forward. Somewhere beyond the ridge the notes of the trumpet soared again. Warner Giddings was putting spit into his work.

Standing Bear lifted his men into the charge with his roaring bull voice. Fifty yards from the hollow Sabin's command to fire pulled the snapper on the warriors. The massed slugs ripped the heart out of the charge. The second volley caught them trying to break away from a tangle of downed men and horses. The third volley drove into their naked greasy backs and bled them still more.

Then the warriors broke for the east side of the valley, screaming in wild frustration. The new grass was covered with writhing men and thrashing horses, while strange red growths, glistening and bright, showed on the green of the grass.

Sabin wiped his face. 'Reload carbines and pistols! Kester! Get in any of our wounded!'

'What about the wounded Indians, sir?'

'You know what to do.'

Kester came back to Sabin leading a stray horse. 'Si Webster and Jimmy Hunter are

237

dead,' he said. 'Denny O'Brien is far gone, sir.'

Sabin saw a trooper binding Jerry LaValle's shoulder. One more wounded.

Manfred Schmidt looked up. 'By Godt that wass fighdting! Now I know why thiss damdt war hass gone on four years yedt. Your men fighdt like berserkers.'

Sabin slid his Colt into his holster. The warriors were rallying a quarter of a mile across the valley.

'Mount!' he said.

'They're licked,' Corby said.

'In a hog's butt,' Kester said. 'This is only the beginning, sonny.'

Sabin set the steel to his bay, watching the warriors out of the corner of his eye. They started forward. Standing Bear had taken a shellacking, but he was far from whipped. Sabin's bay stretched out. Chase Corby raced alongside. The guidon snapped in the wind. 'They're gaining,' he said.

'Thanks!' Sabin yelled. 'I didn't know!'

The war cries came up from the diaphragm and shot through the mouth. Hundreds of unshod hoofs made the ground shake. Then there was a scattered ripple of fire from the hostiles. Slugs chewed into the Texans and their mounts. They sliced through the wagons' tilts and sang piercingly from wagon iron.

The Texans hung low over their horses'

necks and fired across their bodies, emptying the big Colts. The fire slowed the charge and then broke it. The hostiles swept past at one hundred feet, racing to the north, as the Texans leaped their horses over the wagon tongues into the center of the defensive square.

The enclosure was a hell of bucking horses and mules. A man thrashed on the ground, digging clawed fingers into the dirt, while blood flowed from his smashed face. Men jumped away from the hoofs of rearing, excited horses.

Sabin slid from the saddle. About half a dozen men out of the score or more who had left Fort Bowen were still on their feet. Sabin looked about. Then he saw her. She scrambled over the tailgate of a wagon and ran toward him, dropping a long-barreled rifle to the ground. He scooped her up, drawing her face close to his.

'Kathy,' he said. 'Kathy.'

'Who's in charge heah? Dammit! You men theah! Who's in charge, I say?'

Sabin put Katherine down and turned to confront the flushed imperious face of Colonel Clay Bascomb.

'I am,' he said.

Bascomb drew himself up. 'Where is your officer?'

Chase Corby spat at Bascomb's feet. 'Yuh heard him,' he said.

Kester saluted Sabin. 'They're forming on the slope,' he said.

Sabin kneed his lathered bay past Bascomb and looked across the valley. The warriors were stripping down, throwing aside all unnecessary gear and clothing. This time they meant to make damned sure they finished it.

'Heah they come!' Jerry LaValle yelled.

The charge wasn't meant to end in a collision, however. The warriors came on as though shot from a gigantic bow, only to part and race past the wagons, hanging on the far side of their horses. Rifles belched like the ripping of heavy cloth and then the hostiles were gone again, leaving bloody wreckage behind them.

Cobb Howell wiped the sweat from his face. 'I hope thet little bastard Giddings got plumb away,' he said.

Sabin looked at Charlie Kester. 'What do you think?'

Kester fingered a bloody slash on his left cheek. 'We either fight from the wagons or make a break for it.'

'I don't like a defensive fight.'

'There aren't enough of us left for a good killing, sir.'

Cobb Howell stood up in his stirrups to eye the enemy. 'Hellsfire! Our boys will charge hell with a cornstalk!'

'I ain't about to stay here,' Chase Corby said.

'We're damned if we do and damned if we don't,' Kester said.

Clay Bascomb had seen his bright new world crumble and dissolve at the edges. By God, he had always made his way in the battle of life and he wasn't licked now. 'You, suh!' he snapped at Sabin. 'Get those men down into the wagons. I'll take command heah.'

Sabin examined him as though he had just discovered a new breed of lice. 'Where's Marianne?' he asked.

Bascomb flushed. Katherine Williams pointed at the dusty Dearborn. Sabin walked over to the sumptuous vehicle and jerked open the door. He jumped sideways as a pistol poked through the doorway. It crashed, driving flame and smoke past Sabin's face. Then the pale face of Stacy Bascomb appeared. Sabin jerked the heavy pistol from the shaking hand. He pulled Stacy from the carriage. Then he peered into the carriage. She lay on the cushions with an arm across her face.

'Marianne,' he said.

She did not move.

'Marianne!'

She slowly removed her arm. He looked into a face he hardly recognized. Liquor and fear had changed her into someone else. 'It's Sabin Shay,' she said. Then she laughed.

Sabin turned to Stacy. The young handsome face was ravaged with fear. Stacy shakily touched his left cheek. 'She's been that way ever since the Sioux attacked,' he said.

Sabin gripped Stacy by the shoulder. 'Get her out of there. Slap some sense into her.'

Clay Bascomb pushed his way through the silent men. 'I assigned my son to guard his sister,' he said.

Sabin measured him coldly. 'We're going to fight our way through the Sioux,' he said. 'It will be rough enough without anything else hindering us. She'll have to ride with the rest of us—or stay here and wait for them.'

Clay Bascomb tried to stare down the big man facing him but it was no use. 'Stacy, son,' he said, 'do what you can. Her mare is still unwounded. She can ride. She'll *have* to ride.'

Stacy swallowed audibly. He looked from one to the other of the hard Texas faces and groaned. He climbed into the carriage.

'They're massing on the ridge,' Charlie Kester said quietly.

Sabin walked to the wagons. 'Where's your powder stores?' he asked Bascomb.

'In those two wagons. Protected by sheet iron. My own idea, suh.'

'Brilliant,' Sabin said dryly. He studied the terrain. He had noticed that the hostile charges had all converged upon the center wagons in the line. The sloping ground had funneled them that way. He looked behind him. Smoke was smoldering from a wagon in which a fire had been put out. 'Fan up that smoke,' he said.

'You loco?' Howell said.

'Damn it, I want more smoke from that wagon! Plenty of it. A smudge!'

Some of the men fanned the blaze into life. They threw grass on it. Smoke began to drift about the square, making everything indistinct. Across the valley, the warriors pointed and whooped in delight.

'Now what?' Kester asked.

Sabin flapped the wreathing smoke away from his head. 'Get the horses at the south end of the wagon square,' he said. 'Strip those horses down to saddles only. Have every man cut down his gear to his weapons. Everyone here must ride. If there aren't enough horses they can double up.'

'You mean to pull out then?'

'Like the devil beating tanbark.'

'They'll rip us to pieces out there!' yelled a teamster.

Sabin shook his head. 'My men will go last. The rest of you will escort the women.' He looked over his shoulder. The hostiles were still on the slope listening to the harangues of their chiefs. There wasn't much time. He walked to the powder wagons and reached in for a keg. He smashed in the head and dumped some of it on the flooring of the wagon and then ran a thick trail of it to the other wagon. He dumped the remaining powder over the tailgate. Sweat oiled his body and dripped from his face.

Everybody moved swiftly, without talking. The men of the wagon train led their mounts to the south side. A wagon was manhandled from the line. The drifting smoke hung like a pall over the square.

Kathy stood by a clean-limbed claybank. A trooper took her rifle from her and handed her a big Remington. Sabin walked to her and gazed down into the smudged oval face. 'There are six rounds in that handgun,' he said. 'Use five on the Indians.'

'I know what to do with the sixth,' she said.

He bent and kissed her. 'You won't need it,' he said. 'We'll get you out of this, Kathy.'

'And what of you?'

'Every Texas trooper is issued nine lives along with his equipment. You worry about yourself.'

She watched him walk away through the smoke. The butt of the big Remington sixgun was slippery with cold sweat. Suddenly, for no reason, she spoke aloud. 'I've got nine lives too, Sabin Shay,' she said. 'I'm from Missouri.'

Sabin gripped Todd Shafter by an arm. 'Shafter,' he said, 'you talk a lot and you were a troublemaker back on the Pease. But you've got guts.'

'Thanks,' Shafter said sourly.

'Go with the women. If they get cut off, you know what to do. But damn it, man, wait until the last minute. I know how you can shoot a handgun.'

Shafter nodded. 'I was aimin' to do it anyways,' he said heavily. 'I had to do it to one sister back home when the Lipans burned the old ranch. They got the other one—'

Stacy Bascomb had helped his sister from the Dearborn. She swayed in his shaky grasp. He led her to her mare. She stood there resting her head against the horse. Clay Bascomb looked toward the hostiles. 'It won't be long now,' he said, almost as if he were thinking of something else. The old man seemed to have all the guts in the family.

The smoke had thickened as the wind had died away. The warriors sat their lathered mounts, waiting. The chiefs had stopped talking. Sabin took a lucifer-block from his pocket and walked close to the powder wagons. He glanced back over his shoulder. They were all ready.

Then the warriors kneed their paint ponies into a walk, coming down the ridge. The pace picked up, faster and faster. Sabin wet dry lips.

'Get ready!' he called.

The warriors lifted into a trot. *'H'gun! H'gun! H'gun!'* they shouted. This charge would finish the fight.

'Move out beyond the wagons!' Sabin ordered.

He could hear the hurried movements behind him. The hostiles were a hundred yards away. Sabin broke a match from the block and dropped the block into the first wagon. Seconds ticked past before he lit the match and touched off the block. It flashed into life, hissing angrily as the powder caught hold. Sabin turned and ran for his life.

Racing across the smoke-filled interior of the square, he saw Marianne Bascomb break away from Stacy. He made no effort to catch her. She slid from her mare and ran through the smoke, back to her once shiny Dearborn. Sabin yelled. She scrambled into the carriage.

Sabin looked at the wagons. Smoke drifted from them. The hostiles were no more than fifty feet away when a shattering crash broke from the first wagon. The big wagon folded outward like a house of cards. A wheel sailed upward as though shot from a sling. Then the powder kegs in the second wagon let go. Sabin staggered as the blast of air drove him toward his bay. He was up in the saddle when he saw the heavy wheel smash into the Dearborn. Then he raked the bay from head to rump with his spurs and shot out of the smoke as though the powder explosion itself were propelling him.

Behind him the front ranks of the hostiles had been laid flat as though by a giant scythe.

Screaming, powder-burned warriors shielded their heads from the stamping hoofs of maddened ponies. Fire raced across the trampled grass. It licked up the tilts and bows of the other wagons, forming a blazing square of vehicles.

Sabin reached his racing men. 'Hellsfire!' yelled Cobb Howell. 'Yuh shore do things in a big way, Cap'n Shay!'

'We aren't out of the fire yet!'

There was tough fiber in the warriors of Standing Bear. A group of them had circled the flaming wagons. Now they cut in on the handful of Texans who rode between them and the civilians. The screaming warriors bunched for the smash-through. Sabin was alongside Chase Corby. He arm-signaled. The Texans turned to follow the guidon. There was a crash as Texan met warrior. The shock of horse against horse stopped forward movement and the fight broke in a circling quadrille of death. Jonas Gilpin disappeared in the smoke with an arrow jutting from an eye. Jerry LaValle got his death stroke from a pipe-ax. The fight whirled across the flats, a wild kaleidoscope of feathers, greasy bodies, flashing weapons and dusty blue uniforms.

Sabin smashed the face of a buck with a shot from his Colt. Two more went down beneath him. Then he was beyond the fight with an ax slash across his left shoulder. He saw Chase Corby go down with a slug in his belly. A squat buck raced in and snatched the guidon, shrieking in triumph as he raised it. It was Standing Bear.

Sabin closed in behind the chief. Something warned Standing Bear. He turned, couching the lance pole of the guidon and driving his pony toward Sabin. Sabin thrust out a hand to grasp the pole. Their horses met chest on, dumping both men down on the trampled grass as the fight tore past them and shredded down a slope.

Standing Bear hung onto the guidon. Sabin smashed at him with the barrel of his pistol. Then the chief recognized him. He let go of the pole and whipped out a knife. Sabin gripped the knife wrist and forced the arm up. The warrior's fingers probed for Sabin's eyes. He dropped the Colt and rammed his right fist home into the lean belly of Standing Bear. As Standing Bear doubled over, Sabin gripped him by the throat. They stood there in Graeco-Roman tableau, straining against each other. Then Standing Bear dropped the knife and twisted sideways for a hipthrow. Sabin hooked his left arm about the corded throat and drew the greasy head close. He put the pressure on until he felt the burly chief weaken. Standing Bear sagged to the ground, pawing for his knife. Sabin threw him aside, let him snatch up the knife, and then kicked him in the face.

Sabin picked up his Colt and fired from five

foot range. Standing Bear doubled over and lay still.

Sabin looked about. The warriors were kicking up dust to the west. A handful of Texans were left. Manfred Schmidt rode toward Sabin and saluted him with a reddened blade. 'Vat are your orders?' he asked.

'Got none,' Sabin said.

'It wass a goodt fighdt.'

'I'm sick of killing.'

Cobb Howell spat. 'There ain't enough of us Texans left for a good killin'' he said.

Charlie Kester slid from his horse. 'The old colonel is dead,' he said. 'Stacy is gone. Took off over the hill. You want us to get him?'

Sabin shook his head.

'The girl is safe,' Kester said.

Sabin wiped his face. He handed the guidon to Howell and walked up the slope to her. Katherine ran to meet him. She placed her head against his chest and clung to him as though she'd never let him go again.

CHAPTER TWENTY-SEVEN

Sam Nelson's wagon train was ready to roll west. The long common grave on the slope had been dug and filled with the bodies of the dead. The emigrants and the soldiers were gathering for the service. A trooper squatted patiently at his key beside the silent telegraph line. Sabin stood beside Katherine Williams looking down at the shrouded bodies of his men, wondering what had happened to little Warner Giddings. The poor kid had vanished into the hills as though spirited from earth.

'Get on with the service,' Sabin told Blalock Lott.

The ageless Biblical words cut across the fresh wind and then there was silence. Blalock crumbled earth into the grave.

And then, suddenly, the telegrapher gave a shout. The people turned to stare at him. His key was clacking briskly. He yelled and stood up, cupping his hands about his mouth.

'Lee surrendered at Appomattox Courthouse six days ago! The war is over!'

There was an emptiness in Sabin Shay. Todd Shafter simply walked away down the hill. He had lost two brothers at Perryville.

'It is the will of Almighty God,' said Blalock Lott.

Sabin caught the guidon as the wind blew over the staff. He ripped the tattered guidon free from the staff and dropped it into the grave. His men were down there, together as they had been since the days on the Pease.

Lieutenant Degnan hurried down the slope to the telegrapher. He checked the message he had received. Then he came up the slope again. He said, 'Shay, my orders are to escort the emigrant train to Utah.'

'Why tell me, sir?'

Degnan grinned. 'This may sound silly, but I'd like to have you and your men come along.'

'Well I'll be damned,' Sabin said, and remembered to smile back at Degnan. 'I'll see how the men feel about it, sir.'

★   ★   ★

The grave was filled. The wagons rolled west. Cobb Howell whistled Sweet Evalina as he cantered past Sabin to take up his position as lead scout. The small escort of troopers had spread out to cover the wagon flanks. In the dust you couldn't tell a Yankee from a Galvanized Yankee.

Sabin squinted through the dust. A familiar figure was driving a wagon at the head of the column. Sabin spurred forward and drew his bay to a walk beside the wagon. He stepped from the bay and sat down beside her, taking the reins from her brown hands. She smiled and leaned against him. Somewhere a prairie lark bugled down the fresh wind.

'It's all over,' Sabin said.

'Yes,' Kathy Williams said. Dreamily she added, 'I've asked Blalock Lott if he can still perform the marriage ceremony.'

'He can,' Sabin assured her. 'I asked him twenty minutes before you did.'

251